$15 U.S.

THE
REAL
ILLUSION

THE REAL ILLUSION

TWENTY-ONE STORIES

Simon Lane

ABINGDON SQUARE PUBLISHING
New York

Also by Simon Lane

Le Veilleur
Still-Life With Books
Fear
Boca a Boca
Twist

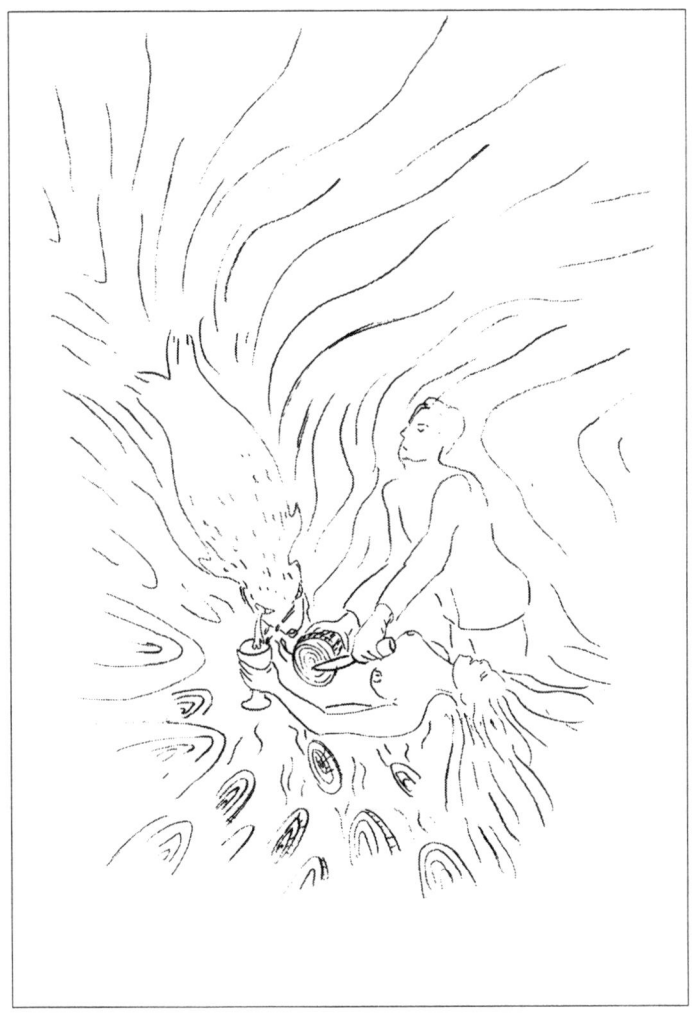

Illustrations by Tunga

The cover drawing, by Tunga, is an illustration for "London: The Correct Manner." The artist has produced a limited edition of ten lithographs of this drawing as well as his illustration for the short story "The Forecast" to accompany publication of THE REAL ILLUSION.

Copyright © 2009 by Simon Lane
All rights reserved.

Except for brief passages quoted in a newspaper, magazine, radio or television review, no part of this book may be reproduced in any form or by any means, electronic or mechanical, including photocopying and recording, or by any information storage and retrieval system, without permission in writing from the publisher.

Copyright © 1996 Louis Vuitton Malletier, for
"London: The Correct Manner"

Artwork © 2009 Tunga

Design by Brian Pilliod

The Real Illusion
is published by
Abingdon Square Publishing Ltd.
463 West Street, Suite G122
New York, NY 10014
www.abingdonsquarepublishing.com

ISBN 978-0-9823480-2-4
Library of Congress Control Number: 2009908690

First printing: September 2009
Printed in the United States of America

therealillusion21stories@gmail.com

ACKNOWLEDGEMENTS

Most of these stories originally appeared in one or other of the following periodicals: Bomb Magazine, The Quarterly, L'Ennemi, Les Episodes, Hors-bord, Paso Doble, lo Spazio Umano and Textuerre. "In New York" and "May", extracts of which appear in this anthology, were published in their entirety by Golden Section Books, London.

"London: The Correct Manner" was published by Louis Vuitton Malletier as part of its "Carnet de Voyage" series. Grateful acknowledgement is made for permission to reproduce the text in this anthology.

My thanks to Gérard-Georges Lemaire, who has edited my work since 1983 and is responsible for the publication of many of the stories contained herein; to Betsy Sussler at Bomb Magazine; to Juliet Chalk; to Barbara Leary; to my other half, Guy Lane; and to Shaida. Special thanks to Brian Pilliod for making things happen.

And, to Tunga: another collaboration sees the light of day.

SIMON LANE

ILLUSTRATIONS

Los Angeles	6
London: The Correct Manner	28
The Vinkristine Saga	92
The Forecast	120
The Art of Reading	134

CONTENTS

1. In Rio de Janeiro — 3
2. Los Angeles — 7
3. Morning in Mexico — 15
4. In New York — 23
5. London: The Correct Manner — 29
6. May — 37
7. The Slapshield Saga — 43
8. The Vinkristine Saga — 93
9. The Devil ain't Bad, Either — 107
10. When the Colonel Dies, Christ will Disappear Forever — 111
11. Between Geography and Science — 115
12. The Forecast — 121
13. The Formalist — 129
14. The Art of Reading — 135
15. The Renewal — 139
16. The Respectable Lady — 143
17. The Art Dealer — 147
18. Uptown, Downtown — 151
19. The Real Illusion — 155
20. Beauty and the Beast — 159
21. The Hostage Returns — 167

For Betsy

"Deus é bom mas o diabo tambèm não é mau"
(God is good but the devil ain't bad either)

Fernando Pessoa, *The Book of Disquiet*

IN RIO DE JANEIRO
2008

I am in Rio de Janeiro. I came here to spend a month. That was seven years ago. Almost to the day. No one ever says, "I am going to Rio de Janeiro for seven years," but people like to exclaim at parties, "I came for a visit and just look how long it's been!" Well, it doesn't feel long at all. This place is in my blood and my blood is in this place. All over it, in fact. I have died and been reborn on various occasions; here, elsewhere. I suppose I have had a big life, whatever that means. Making luck while tempting fate? Possibly. I am fifty years old, I have used up time and I have too much time: all the time in the world. A day is an eternity, a life the simplest of epitaphs. I am a reflection of my own inflated modesty, an ambulant paradox surviving on love, red wine, blue sea, the patter of rain on my forehead, or a burst of sunshine as it lends shadow to a giant mango tree: a toucan squawks on a high branch, taking flight all of a sudden so as to show off its scarlet tail-feathers, the reddest red possible; a monkey robs a banana from the kitchen table and is chased out by a dog I have never seen before; a lizard the length of a pool cue rests immobile, poised, on the terrace; yet nothing really stops in this house on the side of a mountain, whose peak changes shape at the turn of the head. Nature will never need saving, she can look after herself. And me? My emotions have

THE REAL ILLUSION

found a home in this place in order for my thoughts to take shape. I am therefore I think and I think in one language even if I speak and write in others, the language I assumed by default and which I use to satisfy my need to describe the world, happily deluded by the impossibility of the task: English! The universal language of the alien! The necessity of creating fiction has ebbed for now, I have become more of a hapless witness than an instrument of my own, projected imaginings, propelled as always by the most curious curiosity, my guide, my tempter, not the curiosity that killed the cat, rather the fascination of a busy soul in a busier orbit. As for cats, in Brazil they have seven, not nine, lives, for a reason yet to be explained to me. Someone in London, whose drink of choice I forget, once said, "We're the kind of people for whom the light at the end of the tunnel is the oncoming train." Well, I've been in tunnels; been caught in a shoot-out; seen bodies by the road, a parachutist fall into the sea; and I've felt myself dying, attended by nurses, smiles, syringes. I suppose I should be more careful, but then I am not a cat. When it's time to die, the battery will run out and the clock will stop, but it will still tell the truth twice a day at least. I won't go quietly either, I am hoping for light music in the background. I am just a writer but writing calms the nerves, offering an eye of a storm in which to observe life's tragedies, banalities, beauties. I am calm as I write this, even the sea through the window appears to have stopped now, while the sky is an even blue, unusual for this dot, or spot, at which the overheated landmass of South America often meets the air of more southern latitudes in a pointed line, like the noses of a gang about to have a fight over a girl or some money. Last night, the house shook and flashes of lightning came down onto the *favela* nearby as if in response to all the bullets and red tracer fired off into the sky at a helicopter; or just for fun, dizzy complement to *Carnaval* fireworks. Yes, pleasure should be taken seriously too, for seven days, seven years, seven lives, more even. Life is not short, not short at all, just the right length, longer than a lizard, shorter than a silly dream, more like a piece of string plucked from the cobbles of the street you happen to be

IN RIO DE JANEIRO

on, suitable for wrapping any gift, large or small. Writing it all down is another question, any perception of truth being truly imperceptible within the greater sphere. As for the answer: I didn't stay on for seven years because I thought it was simply a good idea, I stayed on because all of a sudden time came to a stop... without so much as a whimper.

LOS ANGELES
1997

I am on a platform above a desert. In the foreground, green AstroTurf. In the distance, a slice of blue ocean, severed by a neon sign: PACIFIC SANDS MOTEL.

I am in Los Angeles. No. I am not "in" Los Angeles. I am "at" Los Angeles, for Los Angeles does not exist, it is a mirage meeting its own reflection, a hall of mirrors leading to the mountains and beyond. In fact, I am "on" Los Angeles, floating, three metres above the ground, on stilts, in a room numbered 26: telephone, television, mirror, Formica, plastic cups, thick carpet. Large bed.

This is my sentence: to be "in" Los Angeles, even though Los Angeles does not exist, even though nothing and no one is "in" anything under this strange, blue canopy. I have come to work, but the work does not come to me. The work is a conundrum, a chain of telephone calls to organise a documentary on horror films for European public television. I am "doing" a horror documentary and the horror documentary is "doing" me. All I am really doing is trying to make myself understood over the telephone. Dylan Thomas called it "the barrier of a common language". I don't even call it a common language.

I call the Director's Guild and I get the names of the film directors needed for interview. I don't know the directors, I don't know their films. And I am producing a documentary on them. I have as little interest in the directors and their films as their agents have in me. I occasionally see their names advertised on the sides of buses and I imagine them doing what I am doing, living a life, glancing at a sunset,

THE REAL ILLUSION

adjusting a smile in a tired mirror. To be perfectly honest, I have a fear of horror films. They frighten me.

I am being paid to be in, or on, or at, Los Angeles, but I have little idea what I am doing. I want to give the impression that the documentary is based on only one director, to increase my chances of organising the gig and getting back to Paris, where everything is easy and explicable and naturally complex. I am not a good liar but lying seems easier here. If Los Angeles is a place, then it is built for the purpose of deception.

Are you interviewing any other directors?

No.

Why am I being paid to be in Los Angeles when I know I will spend all the money I earn while I am here? Because I am also writing a script with a German director about love and gangsters. I have no interest in films, in gangsters. And here, even love becomes an abstraction, teasing me as I glance at the large bed.

I step out into the absurd blueness of this place, or collection of places. Why absurd? Because the blueness is predictable and when blueness is predictable you know something strange is going to happen. I walk down the pavement and throw my cigarette into the gutter. A pedestrian stares at me quizzically. Have I done something wrong? People pass by on wheels, large wheels, small wheels, roller skates, they are larger than people in Europe and they have sun tans and short trousers and they look ahead into the blueness of a place robbed of time and of the free cycle of seasons. And I pass them, invisible, a sometime associate producer of European public television, sometime gangster-scriptwriter, who is actually just a poet trying to earn money to buy time to write when he knows he will spend all the money he earns in order to transform Los Angeles from an idea into a place of comfort.

Comfort? A drink. Lunch. I step into a restaurant a hundred metres from the PACIFIC SANDS MOTEL and I ask for a table. A young woman smiles at me broadly as if I were an old friend. She asks me how I am. I tell her. Then I ask her how she is.

Me?

Yes. You.

LOS ANGELES

I'm fine.

She shows me to a table. Soon a young man with gelatine in his hair is standing beside me recounting a list of dishes with impossibly exotic ingredients. Almost immediately, I lose track of what he is saying, there is a lamb on a bed somewhere, something broiled or charbroiled and a sauce of great complexity. Calabrian olives and Japanese seaweed and Hawaiian mushrooms compete for attention in a swirling, stirring monologue declaimed by the waiter with such conviction I am obliged to avert my eyes for fear of distracting him. He must be an actor. Everyone is an actor here. Even the chef is an actor. He is Hamlet and the waiter is Rosencrantz. And I am producing a film which takes place in a restaurant in Santa Monica which will be a horror documentary combined with *Hamlet* in which Ophelia drowns in a lake of minestrone. *The strawberry grows underneath the nettle and wholesome berries thrive and ripen best neighbour'd by fruit of baser quality.*

What was the third one?

The lamb?

I don't know. That's why I'm asking.

Excuse me?

I'll have the beef.

We don't have beef.

The lamb is fine.

Yes, it *is* fine. What would you like?

The lamb.

Fine.

Rosencrantz returns to Elsinore, which is the kitchen, and Guildenstern appears with a Bloody Mary, which has a stick of celery in it the size of a palm tree. I produce my notebook and begin to write of a love that makes my heart turn and become heavy, like a piece of luggage. I look at the nametag. Yes. It is me. Why do I always pack so much and always what I don't need? And why is my heart so heavy? Can I not simply unpack it, push it under the bed, which teases me, travel light just for one, empty moment?

Lunch. Dinner. Lunch. Dinner. Bloody Mary. Lamb. Bloody Mary.

THE REAL ILLUSION

Palm tree. I return to the restaurant which is an auditioning suite for a series of films without end in which everyone acts, even the audience. After a week, I have become an automaton. I have already used up my expense account in telephone bills calling friends and family in Europe and New York, trying to describe a place that may or may not exist.

Can I help you? the young woman asks.

I'd like a table.

Certainly, sir.

When I came here for the first time, you treated me like an old friend. Now that I am a regular, you treat me like a stranger.

Would you like to sit inside? Or on the terrace?

I'd like to sit where I sat last time. Where I can smoke cigarettes.

Come with me.

One night there is an invitation to meet "Arnold". It is a "cigar evening".

What is a "cigar evening"?

People smoke cigars, explains the man who invited me to work in Los Angeles, who is German and a man of energy and conviction and whom I shall call Hans.

What do we do about dinner?

You get dinner, explains Hans.

So it's a dinner.

No. It's a "cigar evening".

A limousine picks me up at the motel. We arrive at a restaurant, which belongs to Arnold, who is a large man from the Austrian mountains who once turned his body into a photograph. This is a private dinner for those lucky enough to be invited who wish to be in the same room as Arnold and smoke cigars. I take my place at a table. A waitress who could be Ophelia appears with plates of lettuce and I drink a whisky. Another waitress, Ophelia No. 2, hands out packets of cigars and everyone opens up the packets and lights them. There are no Cuban cigars, only Dominican cigars, and soon the room is filled with the smoke of a faraway country, rising in the air of a restaurant that is not only staffed by actors but also owned by one.

LOS ANGELES

The man opposite me is a film director. He is trying to smoke his cigar. His neighbour explains that he should cut it first in order to let the air through.

I've never smoked a cigar before, he says.

Everyone, whether they like cigars or not, is smoking. I calculate it will take at least another fifteen minutes before we start our meal. It occurs to me that people here do everything backwards. A stranger is greeted as a friend. And cigars are smoked before dinner. Will I be able to make love to Ophelia No. 2 and then ask her what her name is afterwards? As for Arnold, I eventually shake his hand and introduce myself.

He's smaller than I thought he would be, I tell Hans afterwards.

That wasn't Arnold. That was one of his bodyguards.

So where was Arnold?

He didn't make it.

If he didn't make it, why were his bodyguards there?

They're always there.

He must be very important to have bodyguards watching over him even when he's not there.

Arnold is very important.

The next morning, I enter a bookshop. I have decided to take a break from the horror documentary and from the film script and read books instead. Chairs have been placed in rows at the back of the shop and people are sitting down and talking excitedly. A signing is about to happen. On a poster I see the book advertised: STOP BEING MEAN TO YOURSELF. Underneath it is a subtitle: A GUIDE TO SELF LOVE.

I am looking for the third volume of Lawrence Durrell's *Alexandria Quartet* and while I do so I glance at the audience. Presently, the author appears and stands before them. Questions are asked of her. I have now located *Mountolive* and I step towards the cash register.

Does that mean I can be mean to other people?

The man at the cash register hands me the book and my change.

No. Not at all. Loving yourself is the first step to loving others.

THE REAL ILLUSION

I see.

Back at the motel I pour a large whisky and read some Lawrence Durrell. "A man is only an extension of the spirit of a place," he writes. But if the spirit of a place is elusive or nonexistent, how do I go about extending myself? I see my body stretching like a shadow near sunset, extending towards a lost spirit and I realise that I have become completely disorientated in this place of infinite blueness. I am truly floating now. Not even an awareness of the cardinal points is of use to me. Everyone is acting, I am a member of an audience which has been told how to behave at key moments in a drama without end and Los Angeles is falling slowly to my feet, an earthquake has come to claim it and I am slipping silently through a crack in the pavement.

There are no messages for me. There are never any messages for me. The man behind the bulletproof glass in reception is Chinese and speaks very little English. Each time I return to the motel, the same dialogue repeats itself.

Any calls?

Yes.

Who were they?

I don't know.

There is nothing I can do about it. There is nothing I can do about anything. I'm just existing on a platform above Los Angeles. Time moves slowly and I move slowly with it. I am becoming completely abstracted from myself, I am watching an English poet as he goes about the task of being in a place. I turn on the television. A young man is explaining how it was that his daughter was shot through the head by her friend. They were playing at the friend's house one day. The friend's mother had a boyfriend who was an FBI agent. He left his handgun on a table. The friend picked it up and the cartridge of bullets fell out onto the floor. She assumed the gun wasn't loaded but there was still a bullet in the chamber. When she picked it up and pulled the trigger as a joke it blew her friend's head off, so she didn't have a friend anymore, she just had a gun without any more bullets in it.

I turn off the television. The telephone rings. I am invited to a party.

LOS ANGELES

It is forty-five minutes away by car. But I don't have a car. I take a taxi. The driver does not know where he is going. He embarks on a monologue as he enters the freeway, a diatribe against pollution and automobiles.

All these cars. It's terrible. It's not good for the world.

Does Los Angeles have a spirit? I ask.

I don't know, he replies. I come from New York.

We turn off the freeway and drive through the hills. To the north, the city spreads like a map, its folds made indecipherable through a haze of smog and sunlight. Eventually, the driver finds his way and delivers me to the right address. When I get to the party, I am given a huge plastic beaker of tequila Margarita. I stand beside the pool and look at everyone. After a while I meet a beautiful woman who tells me she has made a documentary on Pier Paolo Pasolini. Another woman tells me she is producing a documentary for CNN on war photography that will have an audience of fifty million. I mention the Crimean War, the Franco-Prussian War and the video footage of American fighters in the Gulf.

How do you know all that? she asks.

I am thinking of Pasolini, that he was a poet and a soldier, which Sir Philip Sidney said are the only things for a man to do. I can't imagine how it is that I know of things. What do I know, anyway? I drink the Margarita and the woman who invited me to the party tells me I can go home now.

Now?

Yes. Lisa can give you a ride.

OK.

My stay is coming to an end and Hans is to take me out for dinner. But he's working. I go for my final, solitary dinner in Los Angeles to the restaurant on the corner.

Inside or outside?

Same table, please.

I drink too much. I go to a bar and start talking to a young woman who turns out to be the barman's girlfriend. Then I go to a pool hall.

THE REAL ILLUSION

I approach a man and ask him if he would like to play eight-ball.

I'll beat you, he says. One-handed.

I beat him. He racks up another game. Then he beats me. He seems happier. I return to the motel and pack. The next morning, I walk down the street to buy a coffee. Over the Hollywood Hills, I see a huge white circle in the sky. It is a vapour trail from an aeroplane. What could it mean? The aeroplane moves into another part of the sky and describes an S. I step into the café and buy a newspaper. Then I take a seat outside. In the newspaper is an article about a young man on death row who murdered his lover, cut up the body and threw it into the East River.

I thought I was in a Roger Corman film, he says at the end of the article.

As I return to the motel I see that the S is not an S at all, but a 5. Hans comes to pick me up.

Ready? he says.

Yes. Hans, why has a plane made a "fifty" in the sky?

It's Arnold's birthday.

I see.

We shake hands at the airport and I give Hans the article from the newspaper.

Here's your documentary, Hans. A murderer who thinks he's an actor in a horror film. What could possibly beat that?

I don't know, Simon.

An actor who turns his birthday into a smoke ring?

MORNING IN MEXICO
1993

"We talk so grandly, in capital letters, about Morning in Mexico. All it amounts to is one little individual looking at a bit of sky and trees, then looking down at the page of his exercise book." - *Mornings in Mexico*, DH Lawrence.

And here I find myself, a part of "Morning in Mexico", looking down at my exercise book on the terrace of a house in Oaxaca, a city that Lawrence and so many other writers found, and still find, so conducive to the solitary art of scribbling. And, whatever I happen to write, it still amounts to the same thing, even though Oaxaca is now a little bigger than when Lawrence lived here and even though I am probably a little taller than he was.

My "bit of sky" is expansive. I have more light than anyone could possibly need and I also have some trees, one of which rises up some sixty metres into the sky beyond the walls of this house, giving shade to the seminary next door and towering at night, a cloud of green which, when struck with moonlight, appears as a mute witness to the passing of the centuries, to the complex, enigmatic and violent history of what is now Oaxaca de Juarez. I like this tree. It has endured the rigours of time, the earthquakes, the sieges, the occasional bolt of lightning. It puts everything into perspective, not least myself, an alien being wrestling with a common problem: how to describe this place?

DH Lawrence did a fine job, of course, although I would have to talk *grandly* of this particular morning, which seems as if it could last forever but which will, eventually, become a shadowless thing, a

THE REAL ILLUSION

little too hot for ambling about but just about perfect for my first sip of mescal. I have my friend, Rodrigo Diaz Cervantes, with whom I can discuss the finer points, the never-ending details, of that terrifying, transparent liquor: yes, a thimbleful would most certainly put Morning in Mexico on a grand scale, but I will have to postpone such a diversion until at least halfway through this little exercise. One shouldn't rush into things. I nevertheless pick up the fresh bottle of *El Cortijo* and invert it, to check whether there is a ring of bubbles, *"un collar de perlas"*, lining the upturned meniscus. Then I put the bottle to one side, safely beyond reach for the time being on the far side of the table.

DH Lawrence, of course, was not the only author to pass the time of day in Oaxaca, wondering what it was that made the place tick and what made him tick so well within it. This strange, bearded figure was always the unknown quantity, revelling in the hidden splendours of his surroundings, the more exotic, as far as he was concerned, the better he could pursue his work. There is a charming lady who runs a shop down the road, whose father, it seems, was his doctor. Yes, even mythological characters need a good doctor in Oaxaca, one who will obligingly remind them that *"Para todo mal mezcal, y contra todo bien, también!"* I have also learned that the most effective antidote for "amoebas" is a swig of mescal to intoxicate the intruders and a spoonful of sand to blast them to kingdom come. One almost sympathises with them.

What of all the others, that inventory of dusty scribblers who appear from all four corners of the globe, pouring off buses, trains and taxis, notebooks to hand, waiting impatiently to fill those virgin pages with their own views of this place? They will remark, perhaps, upon the greenness of the stone in this Emerald City, the preponderance of ornately decorated churches, the ridge of mountains that so neatly encircles the metropolis; or the mysterious light of early evening when the *Zócalo* comes to life, transforming itself, to the accompaniment of a waltz carried in the air from the imposing bandstand into a large, open theatre in which each passer-by becomes not only a spectator but also an actor of sorts, repeating a role so often played in the past and always to a packed house, so that even the casual tourist finds himself being applauded by a veteran of Morning in Mexico. He looks around carefully and catches his reflection in the face of a complete stranger seated at an adjacent table, who is doing exactly the same thing. "Where are you from?" says the first. "Where are you going?" says the other.

All these people, individually, in gangs or in gaggles, happily pursue their fantasies and are somewhat perturbed to find that their fantasies then pursue them as they walk the streets, linger and loiter, before returning to their hotels or boarding houses in order to compare fact with fiction, the former constantly intruding upon their imagination as they lay down their weary heads and take a rest from the life of a foreign city. And the writers? What do they do? What possible order can they impose on the things they see and feel so that it all makes sense somehow?

Much as I like DH Lawrence, I prefer Aldous Huxley, which is probably letting the side down, although I am still patriotic for someone who has spent a number of years travelling far and wide looking for Oaxaca and, in the process, lost his bearings a little.

Huxley, forever the intellectual, the lofty, myopic genius, sought in this valley high above the sea a transcendental experience, a way of seeing inwardly: his experiments with hallucinogens must have brought him closer to many things, not least some form of understanding of the people who created this spot from nothing long before planes scratched lines in the sky or the strange beings (actually soldiers on horseback) descended from the north. But that's another story.

Huxley's reactions to Oaxaca, well documented in his *Beyond the Mexique Bay*, find resonance sixty years later. "Yes, Oaxaca is a fine place," he declares, "A stately city!"– and Santo Domingo is "one of the most extravagantly gorgeous churches in the world". He was naturally astounded by Monte Alban: "The site is incomparably magnificent. Imagine a great, isolated valley at the junction of three broad valleys; an island rising nearly three thousand feet from the green sea of fertility beneath it. An astonishing situation. But the Zapotec architects were not embarrassed by the artistic responsibilities it imposed on them. They levelled the hill-top ... few architects have had such a sense of austerely dramatic grandeur as these temple builders of the great Toltec tradition. And few have been given so free a hand."

He also had some interesting things to say about DH Lawrence, noting, a little haughtily, that "the attempt to return to primitiveness is both impractical and, I believe, wrong". One cannot be sure that that was indeed Lawrence's intention. There is no mention of mescal in Huxley's reflections, although the author is particularly impressed by the stonework at Mitla, likening it to "petrified weaving", even if "handicrafts" leave him indifferent.

One must take it all, of course, as one takes mescal, with a pinch of salt. After all, Frank Waters, in *Mexico Mystique*, reckons Monte Alban to be only fifteen hundred feet above the valley. I suppose it depends on how you get there. And how tall you are.

For my part, I have never been one for pots and rugs and have no desire to return to the primitive or, for that matter, a house full of bric-à-brac. A reluctant product of an age that someday someone else might find interesting, I acknowledge the fact that I can never integrate myself, that I am forever an interloper, but I am still obsessed by the idea that, in microcosmic terms, we are all equal, a delightful reduction to absurdity of *homo sapiens*, capable of creating and destroying beauty in the time it takes to swig a mouthful of cold beer. What we actually do becomes strangely insignificant when we are taken out of context, held up to the light and briefly examined before being set down once again onto the pavement. It could be confusing. And it is. But I digress: *El Cortijo* just slipped a few inches towards me.

Yesterday, I was reading one of Italo Calvino's last books, *Under the Jaguar Sun*, in which the author alludes to the sensual pleasures of Mexican food while seated at a table in what was once the Convent of Santa Catalina and is now the luxurious Hotel El Presidente. Perhaps I am too epicurean by nature but I find it easier to absorb a strange culture with the aid of a knife and fork or a brass cup than through my sunglasses. You've got to taste it, the point to Calvino's story, which he extends to his relationship with his travelling companion, with whom he becomes "assimilated ceaselessly in the process of ingestion and digestion, in the universal cannibalism that leaves its imprint on every amorous relationship...". Yes, one takes what one can on a visit to Oaxaca and one has to sit on one's suitcase in order to close it when it's time to leave. Mine will contain many things, tastes, sounds, images, odours, bottles, books, my intoxication will linger and I will see everything so clearly the minute the plane lifts from the ground. Oaxaca will become smaller and smaller and I will be able to hold it in my hand, like a postcard, its picture the grandiose, extravagant mountain shaped to fit an architectural fantasy. Then I can say I wish I were there amidst the great Mexican landscape, instead of here, walking the aisles of a distant airport, trying to find my luggage and a spot to smoke a cigarette without being apprehended.

Huxley's fiction (*Eyeless in Gaza*), like that of Graham Greene (*The Power and The Glory*), benefited, unquantifiably, from that landscape, one which was never simply a backdrop but which seeped into the blood of his protagonists, that mixed bag of characters who found themselves so subordinated by the air they breathed and by the breathtaking richness of this exotic land. Both writers should have been grateful for the inspiration and doubtless were, for this is a creator's paradise, twenty-four hours a day or, at least, not just in the morning.

"I do profoundly think" wrote Malcolm Lowry (a different kettle of fish altogether) in a letter to his friend, Juan Fernando Marquez, in 1937, "that the Oaxaquenians are among the most courteous, sweetly gracious and fundamentally decent people in the entire world." Known for his excess, his hyperbole, his waywardness and an almost pathological desire to court disaster, Lowry could have been exaggerating, carried on a wave of emotion, or of mescal, for he was partial to a drop himself. Not a bit of it! He was thrown into the local slammer more than once, so this was hardly the platitude of a well-mannered guest, however welcome, or unwelcome, he may have been. Of all the English writers of the century, he was the one to dig the deepest into Mexico; and he very nearly dug his grave. He found his exegesis here, his *paradiso* and his *inferno*. The *purgatorio* happened, oddly enough, in a cottage in Ripe, Sussex, twenty years later. Dante is everywhere you like to find him.

THE REAL ILLUSION

I am as overawed by this city as he was. I can feel its beauty, I can sense its elusive qualities, but I cannot really get the measure of it or find the means of defining it, which is probably why it impresses me so much. We outsiders from an alien world can be rather self-conscious, we like our teas crossed and our eyes dotted, yet sometimes it is a pleasure in itself not to understand, not to know, to allow an atmosphere that is almost palpable and certainly unique to remain unidentifiable. "Why?" "When?" "How old?" "How much?" are the questions that fill the air, in interrogatory bubbles, above this great valley. And what a delight it is to be told "We still don't know" in answer to another, anxious question related to the orientation of an ancient structure or to the manners and customs of a people who could be friends one day but who would never knowingly give away too many secrets.

I can neither add to nor subtract from it all, from all the things that have been said or written about this place. A modest scribbler, another one, from England, I arrived as a result of a premonition, or a dream. I am staying in a four-hundred-year-old house with its own Garden of Eden, a rich, tropical corner of Oaxaca full of ghosts but also birds, either mating or fighting or trying to do both at the same time, singing and shrieking and screeching in rehearsal for some unsolicited musical interlude or peep-show. Some of them have nested in my study, they occasionally interrupt my work but they never really bother me; they have things to do, perhaps they think *I* am interrupting *them*? We get along quite well, actually, doubtless because we are visitors to the same place. As for the ghosts, they cannot fly away but they seem pretty friendly, pretty harmless for now.

I spend my days in this hermetically sealed paradise, repeating Lowry's refrain to be found on the last page of his novel, *Under The Volcano:*

"Do you like this garden, which is yours? Make sure your children don't destroy it!"

I like this garden, which for the moment is mine: the sky above it is a constant blue; the birds awaken me so that I no longer have to buy a battery for the alarm clock I have long since banished to a cupboard;

the stars appear, on cue, every evening; and the moon changes its shape, from a sliver to a neat circle and back again, so that I might enjoy a different view of it, wondering why it was that man decided to go for a walk on it when it looks so appealing from afar. For all this I am grateful.

And, as for Morning in Mexico, it has now slipped past me. There will be another, which I know, in advance, will be identical to today's, for me to savour tomorrow. Time slips past but if I wish I can stop it by reminding myself I am in Mexico, in Oaxaca. I can then restart my own, twenty-four hour cycle of existence, inaugurating it, in celebratory fashion, with that drop of mescal I promised myself a while ago, to keep the "amoebas" at bay, strictly, you understand, for medicinal purposes.

Be warned, however: the "pearl necklace" is not a definitive guide to quality. Appearances, after all, can be deceptive, which is something for which we should all be eternally thankful.

IN NEW YORK
1982

I am in New York City. It is mid-October. From where I lie I can see the diving boards for the desperate, the launching pads for the last-time sky divers, concrete balconies without rails jutting out from the tower block across the street, cut off from their parent structure by the vertical line of red check curtain that hangs limply from an old brass rail near the ceiling. The sun shines through appropriate gaps so that the passing reflections of pigeons flicker across the sky-blue walls of my room. Over my body is draped a Union Jack, in lieu of blanket, an artless detail, not warm but comforting in a strange way. I have recently, just this minute, awoken from a fitful, twenty-minute siesta, during which twenty-four hours' worth of dreams visited me. I cannot tell you of my dreams; only of my increasing somnambulance. In the room adjacent to mine, in what I should refer to as the studio – the apartment belongs to an artist friend who took me in one day - the song *Love Will Tear Us Apart* is being played, volume setting nine. In that is a story. Above my head and aside from the more obviously practical elements of my room is a painting entitled *The Goats of Good Fortune*, a delightful picture of three such animals, all of whom take it upon themselves to stare down at me sagaciously at all times of day and night. I fancy they act *in loco parentis*, in a manner which hardly belittles the standard set by my mother and father but which at the same time says a good deal for your run-of-the mill goat. There is a spirituality to the ensemble perhaps too obvious to elucidate, numerically speaking at least. Suffice to say that, despite their somewhat close-up, overbearing nature, they stand with authority from their vantage point above me. Rather like the Empire State Building.

THE REAL ILLUSION

Across the street a man is carrying a tuba, ambling along the sidewalk on his way to the Lincoln Center. On his back he carries a spare, wrapped in a black plastic bin liner. Sometimes he is lost from view as buses and trucks head north or south: The Northern Boneless Meat Corporation ("We regulate the fat content of our beef and check it with special instruments"); or Hilldrup Transfer and Storage ("There's smooth shipping ahead of you"). The rain has come now and the umbrella vendors are back in business.

They have stolen the swing scaffolds in order to make loft beds, they have ripped up the grass with the textured soles of their jogging feet, they have sent Frisbees into the trees and filled the air with rap, and they have all come tonight to Washington Square Park to listen to an orchestral concert. The police hover nervously as the *non cognoscenti* mingle in the crowd, picking noses and picking pockets: tempers are flaring already and a large man with a cigar is escorted from his seat, shouting. The musicians, tuxedo and diaphanous-clad, blow their notes into the sticky night, over shadowy heads and wooden stand seats. It's a sight for sore eyes and I stand beside a tree, breathing it all in.

I was walking down the street with a friend one night, Eighth, I think it was, when suddenly, as if from nowhere, a man appeared, running and shouting. Overtaking us, he withdrew a large knife, a Bowie knife, from a sheath attached to his trouser belt and proceeded to point it wildly at two youths who were up to no good in a corner. We stopped dead in our tracks. And we watched. When the two boys saw the Bowie knife they made off down the block, running as fast as their legs would carry them, leaving a half-stolen bicycle violated beside a fence. "I'm going to kill you this time! The pair of you!" screamed the man, chasing them down the street.

The sky is as clear and as blue as it can be. It is early in the morning and the red police building opposite is already in shadow. Above hang the water towers of the buildings on the next block. How childlike they

IN NEW YORK

seem, just round, wooden tanks on rusty scaffolding with conical tops pointing upwards into the New York sky. Buses roll past my window, BONANZA and TRAILWAYS, heading north from the confluence of streets in front of me, their noises mingling, the rumbling, dark undertones of their engines rising above the street and the sidewalks. I think of their occupants, arbitrary combinations of passengers seated together, heading out of town, into America.

The Man With The Bowie Knife is up for murder. On two counts. He is standing quite still, with knotted brow. The jury has deliberated and the moment is suspended. The artist from CBS News, wrestling with the man's expression, stops abruptly. Her pencil is broken. Aggravated by her passion and by her inability to capture the scene in the statutory time limit and fully aware of the tenuous nature of her new, professional position, she reaches blindly for her sharpener. Around her the atmosphere is tense and silent; the entire court has turned its attention to her plight in the soulless vacuum of expectancy. Unaware of this, groping for a sharp implement with which to assuage her needs, she unwittingly grasps Exhibit A, the Bowie knife. Blinded by haste, she now proceeds to sharpen her pencil. Everyone stares. From his own particular vantage point, the defendant looks down at her, his face now blanched with remorse. At last, the artist pauses. She looks up to face the judge and slowly puts the knife down. "Sorry," she says, in a quiet, resonant whisper. "Your Honour."

It is Tuesday, the day for my reading. The walls of the café are plastered with back issues of *Life* magazine and there is homemade cherry cake for sale under a hemisphere of cracked plastic on the bar top. It is a summer's evening and the front door and windows are all open, giving out onto Avenue B and Tenth Street. The master of ceremonies leans towards the microphone and announces my name, rather tiredly. I walk up to where he is standing and then I am alone, staring into the audience. I cough and announce my story: "The Hotel".

THE REAL ILLUSION

They walked into the room and put their luggage on the floor. They stepped into the room and placed their bags carefully beside the bed. They walked into the room and threw their bags onto the floor before throwing themselves onto the bed. After some difficulty with the door they entered the room and placed their cases onto the tartan carpet. They opened the door (with difficulty) and stepped into the room. They ran into the room, hurled their luggage onto the carpet before hurling themselves onto the bed. They walked into the room (calmly) after no trouble with the key and seated themselves modestly on the chairs provided. They ran into the room and began to undress. They dashed into the room, forgot about their luggage and walked over to the window. Leaving the luggage on the threshold, they walked over to the window and gazed wistfully at the sea view. Using an axe, they hacked down the door, stepped through the splintered woodwork and threw themselves onto the bed. After detonating the high explosive they stepped over the rubble that was to be their sea view suite and began to make love on the tartan carpet. They stepped into the room, holding hands. They entered the room, sat down together and lit cigarettes. She blew smoke rings.

I read some more. At the back, near the door, is a delegation from the local Hell's Angels chapter. The ringleader has his back to me but he turns his head to listen and to watch for a moment or two. He seems to like what he hears and he turns back to face his colleagues for a moment, pointing at me with his thumb over his shoulder and then glancing at me now and then in an approving manner. On his epaulettes and around the peak of his cap hang chrome chains, which glisten in the smoky twilight. He is now looking at me and nodding. Now I realise if I can make it here, I can make it anywhere.

There are some rum characters in the Ukrainian bar, just a few blocks south of the café: a Marine veteran, thin and bearded, eyes like Wookey Holes in winter, face weary-wrinkled, cheekbones and temples massacred by fighting and sleep, low coloured bags of Budweiser under his eyelids and the fearsome, deathly drunk leer of one who has knocked on the doors of hell but would rather not talk about it and shoot some

IN NEW YORK

pool instead. "You playin' today, Simon?;" and "Put another quarter up!" after he has beaten me; a smooth and dangerous culinary and narcotics expert who likes to flirt with women already spoken for, a mean man of many means to be trusted with anything less valuable than a plastic cigarette lighter or a recipe for marijuana cookies; an extremely pleasant pool shark my age, who also works for Van Gogh Removals.

I saw a BMW motorcycle chained to a mailbox, late at night. I stared at it for a long time, saw it tearing up the potholes of Sixth Avenue, its chained front wheel twirling the blue mailbox around and around, all those *Great times* and *Miss yous* inside churning and dancing like strangers' laundry in a dryer, cut-up letters and cards confusing the best intentions, bashing against the street as the riderless machine disappeared to that point north where the end skyscrapers kiss at Central Park.

LONDON: THE CORRECT MANNER
1994

I return to London after many lives' absence. I am an outsider now. And I have been commissioned to write about a place that was once home as a guide for tourists. I am bewildered by the new banknotes, the Dukes of Wellington, the eternally youthful Queens of England, pushed towards me through a polite, bulletproof slot at Heathrow Airport. Even the man at Immigration seems foreign to me, rifling through the stamps of my passport suspiciously before slapping it onto the counter and waving me on with a sigh. "Next!" As I ride in a taxi and head for the metropolis, I tell myself that a city is always greater than the sum of its parts. London to me was vast as a child and no less so now.

I take a room overlooking a garden. The London garden is not so much a luxury as a prerequisite; but you don't have to own one to enjoy it. The great parks of London do more than offer fresh air and exercise, they symbolise freedom of movement. In St James's Park, you can stare east to the imposing backdrop of Whitehall or just look at the pelicans. In Hyde Park, assuming the visitor is adept, he may rent a horse and canter in ever-increasing circles. The same person will find no flowerbeds in Green Park, for Queen Catherine had them removed upon learning that King Charles II had selected a bloom within its borders and given it to a milkmaid. The gardens of Buckingham Palace are closed to the public, but occasionally the more curious jump into them and sneak up on the Queen to find out whether or not she actually exists.

THE REAL ILLUSION

I am getting in character: I buy a guidebook on the King's Road and light upon "Historical Pub Walk". After two or three pages, I decide I can do without it, so, when a Scandinavian tourist stops to ask me directions, I hand the book over to him and continue my excursion unaided. *Tack så mycket.* I have never visited the church that stands at the southern end of Church Street before, in Chelsea. I enter through the west door. The building is full of time compressed. In a corner is a commemorative plaque to Henry James. "Lover and interpreter of the fine amenities," it reads, "of brave decisions and generous loyalties." The verger appears as if from nowhere and removes a flower arrangement that obscures the remaining text. He stands some distance from me holding the vase, dripping water onto the old stone floor. "He lived three doors down on Cheyne Walk," he says, with some reverence. I nod, select a postcard from a stand and slip a pound coin into a box marked "Upkeep".

It is a day as clear as crystal; the sharp light and thin, autumn air lend Chelsea great beauty, and me a lightness of step. I continue along Cheyne Walk to the house of Dante Gabriel Rossetti: an eccentric, he buried a volume of his poetry along with his young wife, but later thought better of it and had the poems exhumed and published. We all need to earn a Wellington. This corner of Chelsea was full of scribblers and daubers. Further along, in Tite Street, I pay my respects to Augustus John and John Singer Sargent and, a few doors up, to poor, sad Oscar. I rarely do this, I am not usually the type to stare at buildings and become sentimental about them, but I can't help feeling something stir in my heart as I stare at Wilde's house. "The truth is rarely pure, and never simple. Modern life would be very tedious if it were either, and modern literature a complete impossibility," he wrote for Algernon, in *The Importance of Being Earnest.* He lived for aphorisms and he expired within the weave of hotel wallpaper.

I walk up St James's Street, past Lock's, the hatter. This is my

LONDON: THE CORRECT MANNER

favourite shop in London. People need hats as much as they need books. Or used to. I wouldn't mind being a hatter but I think you have to start young. At least if I were a hatter, people would not say that they preferred my earlier hats, or that they found my later hats "too difficult to understand". There is nothing to understand, or misunderstand, about a hat, although some of Lock's hats caused quite a stir in their day, Lord Nelson's with its built-in eye patch, or the curious, domed creation, designed by William Coke and supplied by Lock's, which later became known as the bowler. Of course, I prefer Lock's earlier hats, but then I am a little old-fashioned.

I am beside the Houses of Parliament under the shadow of Oliver Cromwell. Head bowed, this grim parliamentarian appears almost contrite, while inside the House of Commons, politicians from both sides discuss the "Irish Problem", in which Cromwell played no mean part three centuries ago. Crossing St Margaret Street, I soon find myself among a crowd of statues. Fellow tourists make their way amongst them, their cameras pointed upwards so that each head will be framed some while later by a neat patch of grey sky. Winston Churchill, his back hunched, Jan Smuts, George Canning, Benjamin Disraeli and Sir Robert Peel remain fixed in their own, dense orbit, their piercing stares surveying an angle determined for them by committee. Odd to think they will outlive us all. I look across to Westminster Abbey, now pristine after years of restoration, before walking along Bridge Street to the great Queen Boudicca, that wholesome, Celtic beauty charging endlessly towards the traffic to remind us that England is, after all, a matriarchy.

One night, quite late, I stand at the bottom of Regent Street, transfixed by the statue of Eros in Piccadilly Circus. I have never seen him shine so brightly, his metallic wings reflecting what should be moonlight, were it not for the neon that flashes above his head. For a moment, I watch as he disappears over the rooftops of Shaftesbury

THE REAL ILLUSION

Avenue, flying unhindered through the thick London air. I open my eyes and turn back to the pedestal to find him as he was, pointing an arrow towards the heart of some faraway creature.

As a boy, I was once taken to the Savoy Hotel by my father. The shiny facade made quite an impression on me, it was what I would later learn to be Art Deco, but at the time of early adolescence it seemed like the radiator grille of an outsize Roll-Royce. We had lunch and I ordered fish and chips. My father requested tomato ketchup on my behalf and the waiter brought the bottle. "This is an unpretentious place," my father said. "Most others would have put your ketchup in a silver bowl." My paternal grandfather lived for twenty years in London, from the turn of the century. He recalled firemen racing down Regent Street in horse-drawn carriages as he stepped out of the Café Royal. That was his local and he knew everyone who drank there. I like to think of him taking the table vacated by Oscar Wilde, who also frequented the place.

I am walking down Fleet Street. As I wait to cross the street, the wind appears as if from nowhere and casually turns the pages of a newspaper lying in the gutter. Someone has had an affair with someone; the wind has been whistling the story all morning, spreading the gossip from one corner of the city to the next. Everywhere I go, I hear of it. Later, as I am walking along Piccadilly to the Ritz, I see, on the side of a newspaper vendor's stand, the inscription, "Second affair!" If the party concerned can have a second affair between the morning edition of *The Daily Telegraph* and the first edition of the *Evening Standard*, then he – or she – is leading a busier life than me.

The Albert Memorial is a memorial to death, as well as to Albert. The Victorians were greatly interested in death, so when her beloved Albert died, the woman who gave her name and manners to an age ordered the construction of a suitable *memento mori*. What we currently see shrouded in an outlandish veil of scaffolding is the ghost of a man posing as a building. There is something highly contradictory about

LONDON: THE CORRECT MANNER

it, for its grandeur, although fitting to the time, so manifestly betrays the English tendency towards understatement. The Victorians were a conundrum: they placed a veneer of respectability upon a passionate race and ruled an empire under the watchful gaze of a dowdy widow. They can best be summarised by the epitaph I once saw on a gravestone in Highgate Cemetery: "Not always understood."

I place my hand over the *camera obscura* inside the Old Royal Observatory of Greenwich and watch in fascination as the riverscape passes over it. The recent Canary Wharf ill fits my hand yet, as I half close an eye, I am easily transported to the late eighteenth century, when the Thames was crowded with men o' war, yachts and barges. Near the river is the Naval College, divided so as to afford Queen's House a slice of Thames to look at. I step out into the autumn sunshine and stand astride the meridian. Then I wander downhill to a row of anchors exhibited on a cobbled pathway. These huge objects kept ships in check prior to great battles, but the land holds them fast now, transforming them into strange, imperial ornaments. Unfettered from my past and from mean time, I slip off to the Trafalgar for a pint.

All cities may become, at times, parodies of themselves. Paris might be nothing more, nor less, than an onion seller with a striped jumper and a beret, while London might consist of a black cab, a red bus without a door and a policeman wearing a funny hat. The characteristics and eccentricities of a place form its image, both to the outsider and the native. The things for which London is famous still impress me as much as they do a Japanese tourist. Is it because I am an outsider now or because those things are truly impressive? Is it I or is it the place? Who can say? All that really matters is that a bus without a door gets you not only from A to B but also to every point in between. Do not, however, alight from one without waiting for it first to stop.

The weather always comes as a surprise in England. While every nuance, every degree and every type of cloud and rain is boldly predicted, hinted at, suggested or implicated by the wave of a hand and a smile of resignation, no amount of prophesying can safely prepare the native or the visitor for what might happen, or not happen, as the huge minute hand of Big Ben propels the city forward to an uncertain future. The rain spits, drizzles, pours, showers, lashes, drenches or drowns, depending on its mood, its benevolence, its wrath or general misanthropy. And the sun shines, or shines not, occasionally, in the summer, scorching, so that the newspapers scream for it to stop. Yes, a hot summer will bring as many complaints as a cold winter; but a day that meets the perfect criteria is treated like a gift to be unwrapped carefully.

Regent's Park Zoo is my memory of childhood: it is smaller now that I am bigger, although the giraffe house, with its huge doorways, will always remain a Babel's Tower of sorts, an inquisitive neck reaching up to the heavens. I tour the zoo's precincts, following the paths mapped out for me during my infancy. The penguins, that most human of all species, stride hastily up and down the ramps so thoughtfully constructed for them by Lubetkin, playing out in miniature the polite interweaving of a city crowd, negotiating thin pavements and, by so doing, imitating stockbrokers, or the busy advocates of Lincoln's Inn. The elephants, meanwhile, more relaxed in the bulk of their imprisonment, perform a different ritual: they are the zoo's senior citizens, they gravitate with solemnity to the interiors of the Elephant Club so as to avoid being overheard by strangers.

At three o'clock in the morning, I set off to pay my respects to the fallen. I reach Hyde Park Corner and stare over the traffic to the Royal Artillery memorial. This monument has always impressed me. It is a truly noble and atavistic statement, quintessentially English in its proud modesty. The bronze figure of a soldier, standing vigil on its western side below a white cannon, looks down, his helmet shielding his face, his cape over his shoulder to keep out the rain of war. At this ghostly hour, I feel the weight of solitude and loss, sharing Wordsworth's view

LONDON: THE CORRECT MANNER

of the London night: "Dear God! The very houses seem asleep; And all that mighty heart is lying still!"

I am standing in a pub in Mayfair. The pub is a place where people exchange stories and this one proves no exception to the rule. The barman is talking to me as he pours me a drink. "The tears of a certain kind of seal may serve as an aphrodisiac. A wealthy romantic kept several such seals in a pool in his house in Avenue Road. In order to make the seals cry, his butler would tempt them with copious amounts of fish and then feverishly dice onions under their noses. He would then catch the tears in a bowl and place them on a silver salver, carry them into the kitchen and pour the tears into a decanter, depositing the latter onto a small table in his master's bedroom." "Strange tale, barman," I suggest, taking a sip from my drink. "Oh, it's not a tale, sir. You see, it was my job to collect the tears, as it is now."

Tower Bridge is exactly one hundred years old. Standing on its western parapet, I trace the movements of a lone Beefeater as he patrols the exterior wall of the Tower below me. A heraldic emblem on the bridge with the red cross of St George proclaims the motto *Domine dirige nos*. The Thames spreads before me while to my right rises the dome of St Paul's, hemmed in by modern buildings. The sky is clear, the river dark yet reflective. Later, I take a ride along the Embankment, all the way to Battersea. The once great power station is but a skeleton now; it is being transformed into something, a bridge museum, perhaps. If it is, do not expect to find the old London Bridge inside, for it was sold to an American some years ago and rebuilt in the Arizona desert.

Walking through Belgrave Square, I am alarmed to discover an empty shoe on the pavement. I find myself wondering what might have happened to its owner. I stop a passer-by and ask his opinion. He is a tourist, like me, and is not prepared to comment. He doubtless thinks it is perfectly normal. I suddenly realise he is the Scandinavian

THE REAL ILLUSION

to whom I donated the guidebook earlier, but he fails to recognise me, as he is blind drunk. "How did you get on with the pub walk?" I ask. "Is good. Very good!" he exclaims. "Do you like London?" I ask. "London?" he replies. "London is big. Greater than the sum of her parts. Good hat shop. If old-fashioned." Then he walks off, eastwards, still holding the guidebook tenaciously in both hands. I return to my room to write this final paragraph on London and pack my bags before setting off again, as me.

MAY
1985

It is perfectly still here. You can hear the birds, it is spring now and everything, the hedgerows, clear-misted skies and solid red brick buildings, sits parked in its place. By the canal bridge, a pale blue Triumph Herald rests by the road, rusting in the sunshine and nearer home a woodpecker drills a lofty oak tree, beak on "difficult" setting. We stand by the fence and look towards the noise, ratatattat, ratatattat, and discuss the bird's location. The cat trap hangs unused on the kitchen door, the veteran winter wood lying scratched beside it. Is it time to repaint it? Shall we remove the cat trap now that the cat is dead?

A ewe has produced twins: one black, one white. In the newspaper I read that "investment income surcharge" has been abolished. Outside, rain launders the landscape. The grass now looks greener than ever.

Looking from the top of the picture down to the bottom: Heaven, Cloud, Mist, Trees, Twin Silos, Hay, Fence, Ornamental Plant Holder, Lawn, Duck (1), Lawn, Duck (2), Window.

In the novel I am reading, it says, "I measured love by the extent of my jealousy." In the sky, the clouds move and separate as if to some predetermined pattern. At this point, jealousy fades far into the distance, obscured by nature.

When we were young we were given allotments. One brother had a plot the size of a large billiard table, beside the garage. Another had a plot by the lawn. And I had a plot by the courtyard, bordered by a high red brick wall, which I was later to climb and inevitably fall from. Neither of my brothers was a keen gardener. The first left his plot to its own devices and christened it a "Weed Garden" and the second tended his on an intermittent basis. The attitude I took to my garden was one of sustained yet abstract fascination.

There were two trees in my garden. The first was called "May" and the second, "May Not". For some reason as a child I was wont to hack away at the bark of "May Not". When my mother saw what I was doing, she said, "You mustn't do that. A tree is like a person."

We pass by mustard fields, which spread like a woollen blanket from the asylum at the top of the hill. "I've never seen them so yellow before," my father says, as they move out of sight, away from the car windows. On another road, a mile or so ahead, a man is making his way on foot towards our village. The sun is high overhead; it is midday. The man is unsteady on his feet. "He's from Hatton," my father says. And it must be true, for, as I glance into the rear-view mirror, I can see that he is mentally unstable. Where is he going, then?

A woman in the neighbourhood has killed herself. Why is it always the means of suicide that linger in the mind? The crack of a shotgun, the whiff of powder and the dispersal of flesh fill my thoughts as the noise resounds in the May garden. The landscape then feels quieter for the explosion, a solemn epitaph perhaps for a member of the community who is gone forever; and a reminder to a clerk somewhere to alter the population statistics.

"Which is your favourite month?" my mother asks me as we stand in the snow. It is the beginning of the year and I immediately dismiss January as a contender. "Mine is May," my mother continues, after a pause. "Yes, I think May is mine too," I reply, thoughtfully.

MAY

In the pub I drink Flowers' bitter and meet a man who sleeps in his car. Afterwards, I lie on the grass in the May garden and look up at the sky. Squadrons of silver-grey and droning bombers pass overhead en route from one distant country to another, each hold, each fuselage weighted down with war. In a moment they are gone and the sky is clear again. I have drunk too much beer and seen war instead of weather. Nevertheless, it might well rain later.

One of our neighbours is a patriot. He is also a radio ham. So it is that the Union Jack often flies from the radio mast set in his garden. His politics might be suspect but he is nevertheless an Englishman and his home, despite appearances, is his castle.

The firefighters' motto springs to mind, the legacy of a recent trip abroad. *SERVIR OU PERIR*. How distant danger seems here in the May garden!

I have awoken at dawn today and am by the window, looking at the landscape. It is like an empty house; there are sheets of dew over the hedgerows to keep the dust off and cobwebs on the broken stile. Around three inches above my condensed nose the early morning express charges south through the valley towards London. It's starting to get light now.

Two pink vapour trails score the dawn sky. Who knows when the jets passed or where they went; and at what speed they flew?

Through the sound of birdsong, the vibrant hum of a lawnmower sets my eardrums in motion. The bin fills with cuttings and the smell of freshly mown grass reaches my nostrils. One or two members of my family sit outside, on the terrace, drinking and talking. Could they be discussing the recent suicide, or my mother's plan to expand the flock?

THE REAL ILLUSION

I am sitting outside on the Van Gogh chair, listening to the sounds of the birds. It is late. To my right, a bird makes a chirping sound. It is Saturday night, is that a mating call? I turn my head sharply and put my hand to my neck. No, I don't think it's sprained. I turn my head again, slowly, towards the sound of another bird and back again in response to yet another on my left. And so on. I get the impression there is either one, very agile bird in the garden, or a large number of stationary ones.

Hanging from a branch, rather stupidly, is the monkey nut sock, waving in the breeze idly. It is made of red nylon and there are no nuts in it. If I close one eye and look at it from the right angle, and if the wind happens to catch it from the right direction, and if the wind is indeed strong enough, and if I am not distracted, it looks as though the midday flight from Birmingham to Amsterdam is flying straight into it. The chances of this happening are very slight, however, and for the most part I just watch the netted outline of the sock as it plays with the outlines of passing clouds.

It is not May (in fact there is still snow at the ends of the fields) but I catch a glimpse of something that startles me. *HATTON MAN DIES FUMES THEORY* reads the placard outside a local newsagent. How far theory is from practice!

I am sitting on the Van Gogh chair. It is a Sunday morning and I have a novel on my lap. I look around for a moment, at the flowers and the trees. Why is it that I can name only a few of them, the red and yellow ones by the fence? I open the book and start the job of reading. The words are put together well. I listen to them carefully, hearing my voice pass from one to another as my eyes have done in the garden. Writing and gardening have little in common, but reading a good novel in a good garden is a cathartic experience.

I come across a fire hydrant marker, which reminds me of the crosses commemorating the deaths of Resistance heroes in France. *"... Sont tombés dans le champ de l'honneur..."* and *"...gravement blessés par les Allemands..."* By means of association, the firefighters' motto, *SERVIR OU PERIR*, takes on a different meaning. I ask myself whether patriotism alone could drive me to acts of violence in this enchanted landscape.

The horse in the paddock runs about furiously. A mare cannot be far away. One of the ewes is still in lamb, which is strange. The gestation period for a sheep is five months and she hasn't seen Alexander, the ram, since last October. Sometimes, there is no accounting for nature.

In May, one can only dream of winter, of the reflections of snow flakes, shadowy dots thrown by overhead street light onto the smooth layer of whiteness that lies about. We tread in it, walking in our sleep, and our shoe size is left for some shoemaker to stare at after our passing. The cold grips us and we plod on, into the night.

A cousin pays a visit. He has brought some music and some jokes with him, all neatly packed in a tartan holdall. Before long, he is playing Chopin on the grand piano. I sit on the Van Gogh chair, watching and listening. The telephone rings and I go to it. "This is Market Research. What kind of lager do you drink?" enquires a voice.

I awake to the sound of birds this May morning. They are in conversation. It occurs to me that they could be discussing something important. In the distance, I can hear a rooster. "Cockadoo... cockadoo... cockadoo..." Is he bored? Or does he have a speech impediment?

During a walk, I pass through a village. In the garden of a small cottage is a washing line, its hinged branches pressed against the aluminium trunk in the manner of a Christmas tree tied for travelling. In this position, it resembles Modern Sculpture. I imagine a visitor to the cottage mentioning this to the occupants one day. I also imagine

THE REAL ILLUSION

such an allusion baffling them. Everything has its place and the idea that an aluminium washing line might be suggestive of something strange is not to their liking. I move on, perturbed by my thoughts.

On Duck Pond Lane, the one that leads away from the pub, is a windmill. It is homemade, a telegraph pole with four vanes made of sections of corrugated iron, rusted pieces with crinkled edges pointing emphatically in different directions, away from the dented motor car hub cap which serves as its axle. Despite the fairly strong breeze, which ripples the skirts of the hedges and bullies the uncut grass at the roadside, and despite the fact that the windmill itself does not appear to be leashed, the wheel is perfectly still. It is only the bird-shaped weather vane atop the old Elizabethan silo that dances, disorientated in the wind.

The wind! The wind pushes everything around, rattling the windows and shaking the branches of the trees in the manner of an irate father. It is heard and it is felt but, of course, is only seen by its effect.

The old Elizabethan silo has an S-shaped iron support running through it. So has the railway bridge. These fine constructions have worked for hundreds of years. They are architecture's old-age pensioners, they outlive us all; will they ever die?

The shepherd pays a visit. His two dogs lie in the garden, awaiting instructions as their master discusses matters in hand with my mother on the terrace. I sit on the Van Gogh chair near the kitchen door, my novel before me. At such times, it is hard not to feel at one with nature.

The train that takes me to the country is called "Comet" and the one that takes me back to the city, the "Thomas of Effingham". I could never treat the country in the same way that I do the city. If familiarity breeds contempt, then I doubt I could ever stoop to familiarity in my feelings towards nature. But what I really want to know is who Thomas of Effingham is.

THE SLAPSHIELD SAGA
1993

Dedication

To Gardar Svavarsson and his Wife, Hulda, for receiving us with such
Gracious Hospitality and for Guiding us around the Island,
To Gudmunda Kristensdottir, for the Charm, Elegance and Wit of
her
Being,
To Erró The Image Maker, Host in Absentia, Master of Art,
To Magnus Einarrsson and his Wife, Gyda,
To the Staff of the Hotel Thorg,
To the Man in the White Balaclava, who rescued the
Vertiginous Slapshield as he stood, Dumbstruck, beside the
Dettifos Waterfall,
To Eirikur the Fearless, Driver and Guide, whose prowess at the
Helm of the Red Skiff ensured that The Foursome were the first to cross
the
Hinterland this summer season past,
To Madame Bronski, who so deftly saved Slapshield from a
Fate worse than death (during the Battle of Ice Rock) by dispatching no less
than Twelve Celtic Interlopers with the point of her
Umbrella Stick is this
Slapshield Saga
Dedicated.

THE REAL ILLUSION

THE MISSING SAGA

My dreams in this Land of Light are no less strange than usual. In one of them, for example, I find myself walking over to the mini-bar refrigerator of my room; lowering myself carefully onto my hands and knees in order to inspect its contents, I run my finger over an apparently limitless selection of reflective miniatures before lighting upon a Four Roses. Later, I repeat the process, again and again, until a neat row of empties stretches from my bed to the window. A little addled, I return to the mini-bar and peer inside. It is then that I notice, hidden in a corner, a bundle of Toblerone chocolate-bar wrappers, held together with the aid of a rubber band. Removing the mysterious package and setting it down on the desk, I carefully take off the band and unfold the slippery, aluminium foil-skins. To my astonishment, I find that they are covered in the neat and spidery script of an unknown hand. Could this be, I wonder, the mysterious "Missing Saga", or "Unknown Codex", which has excited and baffled so many scholars throughout the ages? And why is it my name that graces the first wrapper, embossed, and then preserved as a perfect chocolate frottage?

THE SLAPSHIELD SAGA

EGIL SKALLAGRIMSSON

It is July, 1993, and I have just returned from my circumnavigation of Iceland. Prior to setting my own saga onto paper, I take a fresh look at the life and times of Egil Skallagrimsson, as immortalised in Egil's Saga. Criminal and Lawyer, Usurer and Altruist, Creator and Destroyer, this towering figure was a collision of opposites, and the poems which punctuate his meander/maraudings give repeated clues as to the conflicting machinations of his personality, creating for the reader a perfectly rounded and living spirit, which transcends the fog of history. He also had a precocious talent for murder, dispatching his first opponent during a sporting dispute: "Egil ran up (to him) and drove the axe into his head through to the brain." He was six years old.

THE REAL ILLUSION

THE EPIC SPIRIT

In his conversations with Osvaldo Ferrari, Jorge Luis Borges, the great Argentine fabulist and scholar, reveals his passion for the Icelandic Sagas. There are two aspects to them that impress him the most. First, the invention or discovery of "circumstantial evidence" within the narrative, which I take to mean the interweaving of plot and sub-plot, the way in which the two coalesce and the teasing use of detail one may ignore only to the detriment of one's understanding of the tale. In fact, there is no detail to be found in a saga. Every syllable counts. Perhaps it is for this reason that Borges cites the "epic spirit" as the second aspect that so appeals to him, so much preferable, in his view, to the lyric or elegiac found in other literature. The epic, for Borges, is the paradigm. Further on in his interview, he transfers his attention to Hollywood and, in particular, the "Western": "The image of the cowboy is an epic one, even if that image does not correspond to historical reality." And it is true that, in reading Egil's Saga, one detects traits of the latent cowboy in Egil Skallagrimsson:

>Blows battered the shield,
>Blades crashed,
>My hard hand
>Hurled the steel-flash!

THE SLAPSHIELD SAGA

MY PALACE OF WORDS

The multiplicity of Egil's talent ensured his legendary status. He was all that a poet should be, and his verse, with its self-deprecating honesty and timely revelations, demonstrates its importance throughout the narrative as a guide to the inner workings of a dynamic and independent spirit, of a conscience wavering constantly between good and evil. As such it becomes indispensable, expressing, through its clarity and wit, the personality of the anti-hero, as well as the secrets of a vast, palpitating heart:

>From my palace of words,
>From my temple the word tree
Tells its growth tale.

THE REAL ILLUSION

THE HOT SPRING DANCE

The rising, sulphurous fumes of a hot spring envelop a travelling companion, the Composer, Leon Light Air. One moment he is trapped within their shimmering embrace, the next he reappears, a New Man, an Apparition of Musical Abstraction. Notes and Notation appear from his lips, bars of music cross his wrinkled brow, whilst the setting for a Quiet Symphony heads upwards into the clear, blue sky. He removes his spectacles and wipes them with a corner of his Adirondack hunting jacket. Then he turns once again into the bubbling cloud, hopping with one foot, then the other, in time to the gurgling vibrations of the inner earth:

> This is the Hot Spring Dance
> Serenade to The Fallen Warrior
> Concerto in G Flat Minor
> Precipitous Dirge
> For the Dark and Lonesome Tourist.

THE SLAPSHIELD SAGA

THE CRUCIFIX

Down on the beach, the blackened beach, the crucifix rises above the storm tide, its serrated edges, defunct antenna, steps rusted with sulphur sticking out like a warning, strange epitaph for the unknown shadows that stride, forever, from slippery deck to restless shore. Slapshield looks down from the mountain, shrouded in the mist, blown and bullied by the gale, his arms outstretched like wings, his face averted from the stinging rain which flashes across the landscape horizontally, whipping the back of his head so that the lobes of his ears feel heavy with the cold:

> The Ship went down
> No hands were lost
> But its Cargo of Frosted Cod
> Still swims in the Hold
> Below the Sign of the Cross.

THE REAL ILLUSION

LINDARKOT

Lindarkot is a red house perched in the wilderness, halfway across the Interior, stuck within a sea of crumbled lava. It is a safe house, open to anyone. On a table inside is a guest-book; all houses in Iceland have one, they are not blank pages requiring acknowledgement but vital clues to the traveller's passing. They form part of the Icelandic ethos, politely seeking comment, written rather than spoken. Turning the pages of the Lindarkot guest-book, I consider the tome's epic qualities: a line here, another there, scribbled versions of the same story, sagas told from different perspectives. I tell myself that when I return to Vínland I will create my own guest-book, cheating visits to exotic places or inventing other itinerants who pass, from time to time, through the same spot:

I was walking
From One Side To the Other,
The Weather got Worse
The Temperature dropped,
I'd have ended up in a Box
If I hadn't stumbled across Lindarkot.

THE SLAPSHIELD SAGA

THE ICELANDIC SKIES

The Icelandic skies are a startling and beautiful mess, for the heavens seem unsure as to how, precisely, they should go about the task of organising themselves. The Gulf Stream to the south and the Arctic to the north create a meteorological confrontation, which often appears as a battle, at other times a skirmish, and occasionally as a form of reluctant ceasefire. There seems to hang an invisible line in the sky, bisecting the one that runs, north-south, through the earth, that fearsome scar marking the collision of the American and European tectonic plates. Looking up, one often finds cloud of every conceivable type, from billowing cumulo-nimbus to thin cirrus-stratus, yet more often than not, the shape and form of the cloud are impossible to define. It is in this way that the skies seek to make order from the chaos produced by a waft of southern warmth and a rasp of polar air:

No matter how much The Weatherman
Might shake his head
Or raise his arms Upwards
Sideways
Around and Around
He still fails to get the measure of it all.

THE REAL ILLUSION

THE SLAPSHIELD SAGA

Eirikur The Red, at the behest of Gardar, Earl of the East, guides the Foursome through the Wilderness in the Red Skiff, built from Drift-Parts by the Great Thor-ota. Revelation, expectation, expiation. Leon The Lyricker hums the twin-barred refrain of the Answer-Anthem, Slapshield composes runes on the side of the skiff, using an unknown element from his Multiple Swiss Sword, Sharplens records through the mirror that is her inner eye and Tura changes the shape of the landscape with a sweep of a gloved hand:
> She skips across the Lava-Field
> Chanting the Devil-Ditty
> Catharsis, Extrapolation, Revelation
> (Followed by Drinks).

THE SLAPSHIELD SAGA

THE HORSE'S HOOF

The Horse's Hoof, in the east, appears ominously through the mist, the imprint of a giant quadruped as big as the moon, a cloven rift valley one kilometre wide stretching in a horse-shoe with granite cliffs set one hundred metres up all the way around, as far as the eye cannot see. Slapshield looks down at his boots: the laces are broken, the leather uppers sodden and useless, the water seeping through his soles, the moss underfoot ingratiating itself between his holed socks and his pale fuss-fingers. Then he walks on, leaving his own hoof-print and calling out to the Wet and Dead Muses:
>
> We jumped Skiff
> Fully laden
> A Speck of Red
> A livid Tongue
> Wavering in Half-Light.

THE REAL ILLUSION

THE DARK CITIES

Dimmuborgir, "The Dark Cities", a volcanic conurbation to the north, is now roped off, with a series of winding trails, duly arrowed and annotated for the disorientated visitor. Sharp rocks, sculpted as if the day before, provide footholds and backdrops. Presently, The Foursome come across a cleft, an arched recess known as "the church". They step into it, carefully, peering within the gloom for signs and symbols. There are none to be had. Presently, a gaggle of interlopers, tourists probably, clad in coloured garments, some sporting Day-Glo heraldic costume, hiking boots and plastic helmets, step forth from the inner-beyond. "Well met!" cries Slapshield, running the largest of the group through with his Sword Stick. In fact, he does nothing of the sort. He simply fails to respond upon being greeted in their local dialect. "I distrust crowds!" he exclaims, setting out on his own through the craggy aperture and disappearing into the misty, bewildered morning.

THE SLAPSHIELD SAGA

PUFFINS

Puffins are penguins two blocks down the road of evolution, three steps behind the headwaiter. Below-average aviators, their fin-wings are a compromise between sea and air. When nesting, they have a tendency to over-eat and, as a result, after their young have taken off for the first time, they are obliged to diet before following them off the cliff. They have great character, slightly less comic, slightly more exotic than the penguin. Slapshield stared at them for a while through his binoculars and marvelled at their splendid colours. They seemed at home in Iceland. "They can be quite tasty," declares Eirikur the Bird Snatcher, so, before driving off towards another spot, or clot, Slapshield bags one of them and throws it into the back of the Red Skiff:

The Puffin has Breathed Its last
I clove it in Two
With My Sword Stick
(Tweezer Function).

THE REAL ILLUSION

THE BATTLE OF PENGUIN BLUFF

While Slapshield was looking at the puffins, Eirikur engaged in an argument with a bus driver who had held them up on the cliff road, refusing to be overtaken. Icelanders do not lose their temper. In fact, they hardly raise their voices. Sometimes, however, they take it upon themselves to "make a point". It is true that, on weekend evenings, the populace engages in drinking bouts of Odinesque proportions, sharing their horns of beer and accosting one another with words, greetings, entreaties and slappings of the Bum-Shield. But in all that time, Slapshield hardly saw one murder. As for Eirikur the Puffin-Pincher and the bus driver, they were soon shaking hands and discussing the nature of their shared landscape, hoping they would meet again at some later date, on another bluff.

THE SLAPSHIELD SAGA

THE DEVIL'S WORKERS

According to Laurus The Lofty, Volcanic Farmer, Shepherd, Smiling Viking, it is all the product of the Devil's Workers, that tireless band of helpers whose unceasing toil has fashioned and continues to fashion the lavascape. Laurus took the Foursome to the Devil's Hole and threw a rock into it. Slapshield leaned forwards, as close as he dared, cupping his ears from the terrible wind. But he heard no drop, no echo, no fall; the rock fell and fell and continued to fall, through a hole in the magma, and did not stop until it had reached Australia. "Did you hear it?" exclaims Laurus, with a mischievous grin:
"Did you hear the rock fall?"
Four heads shake,
"Of course you didn't!
It's the Devil's Hole!"

THE REAL ILLUSION

LAURUS THE LOFTY

Laurus is an Eager Man, ebullient, irrepressible, charismatic. Of great charm and energy, this towering figure, a little gaunt, or thin, strides his lava fields in search of lost lambs, plucking them by the scruff of the woolly neck and returning them to the fold. His largesse and laconic spirit make him an Indispensable element to the Icelandic Sagas. He is everything that Egil Skallagrimsson might have been, had that great bumbling figure learned to curb his emotions a little. Slapshield and Laurus the Lofty are to be seen climbing the volcano, although Laurus, despite his seniority in years, is soon a good fourteen skiff-lengths ahead of the Vínland poet. When they reach the top, the latter is breathless, the former ready to dance across the ice-shield:

"All that you can see Slapshield
Or at least half of it
Is my grazing
And you know who made it all
Don't you?"

THE SLAPSHIELD SAGA

OLOF, WIFE OF LAURUS

Olof is a kindly woman, who for the past two decades has recorded the weather and transmitted the good news, as well as the bad, to a distant station, every three hours, around the cold and clammy clock. Mother of eight, wife of Laurus, she is a woman of stature. Slapshield gets the impression that the Icelandic people are one family and he is hardly mistaken, for it is, after all, Olof's brother-in-law who will later perform the ritualistic forecast on the television, for the benefit of all. And the weatherman is also a poet of sorts, an Egil Skallagrimsson in sheep's clothing:
>   ... From the tip of my tongue
>   So much tumbles!

THE REAL ILLUSION

THE VÍNLAND SAGAS

The Vínland Sagas consist of the same story told twice. The first is the Graenlendinga Saga, set down in the late Fourteenth Century, whilst Eirik's Saga can be traced to two vellum manuscripts, one dating from the early Fourteenth and the other from the late Fifteenth Century, so that there are two apparent versions of the second rendering of the story. The medieval scribe, Hauk Erlendsson, who was also a descendant of Thorfinn Karlsefni, leader of the colonising expedition to Vínland, shortened Eirik's Saga and stressed his ancestor's role in the affair. Erlendsson was a great writer and a stylist. A good many contemporary writers could learn from him, but it is more than likely they would consider him "old fashioned". What matters is that, in fusing legend with history, the saga writers transcended the mythological. There is nothing mythological about Iceland, for its culture can be said to be:
Neo-Historic-Viking-Runeful
With just a hint of the
Nether-Beyond-In-The-Lava
About it.

THE SLAPSHIELD SAGA

TWO MIDNIGHTS

I see time come to a stop here in my room at the Hotel Thorg. The travelling alarm clock on my desk seems to slow with each revolution of its luminous minute hand, while the huge clock face on the building across the square appears, from here at least, to be stuck, perhaps even turning backwards in the hope of recapturing some lost moment. There is no darkness, of course, so I can be forgiven for thinking that I am caught between two poles, two midnights, forever condemned to wait for the dawning of a day I now know will never come. This is a strange and chilling thought, but I should count my blessings, for I now realise that I have all the time in the world to complete the Slapshield Saga.

THE REAL ILLUSION

SOME BIOGRAPHICAL INFORMATION

I was born sometime in the mid-Twentieth Century in or near the village of Lipp, at that time free of the Viking yoke. I travelled to Vínland and settled there, writing books and scribbling poetry on walls, establishing a reputation as a scribe and raconteur. Apart from a series of marauding trips and hunting excursions to Iceland, not much else is known about me, although in the early Twenty-first Century, I am to be found in Paris, performing my work with the celebrated composer, Leon-The-Epic-And-Elegiac-As-Well-As-Lyrically-Oriented:

I've seen the Light
I've seen the Dark
I have scars on my knees to prove it
My hair is grey
My skin is thick
And my prose is short but lucid.

THE SLAPSHIELD SAGA

EIRIKUR'S QUEST

The thin Viking, Eirikur Sharp Nose, weaves his way up the mountain. In the winter, he deflates the mammoth tyres on his skiff and rides the glacier as if born to the task. His navigation aids include dead reckoning by radio and a "membrane sense" for crevices, gorges and fissures. Eirikur's dream is to traverse The Graenlendinga Glacier and he is looking for sponsorship. The (Royal) Society for the Prevention of Cruelty to Skraelings has already replied in the negative, but he is undaunted:

> The Great Thor-Ota
> Stands Proud and Sure
> A Fighting Skiff
> Be-Wheeled
> In the Wheelderness!

THE REAL ILLUSION

SKRAELINGS

Skraeling was the name the Vikings gave to what Columbus and his cronies would later call Indians, although it is true that it was also the name given to the indigenous inhabitants of Greenland. The later discoverers of what would one day be America thought they had encountered the eastern seaboard of the Indies. And the Vikings? What did they think when they came upon this continent, with its fish-full rivers, moderate climate and profusion of wild grapes? That it was paradise, perhaps? "Skraeling" can be translated as "wretch". But it was these wretches who ultimately saw off the Viking settlers from Vínland. According to one source, the skraelings were members of either the Micmac or Boethuk tribes. Whatever they were called, they must have been excellent warriors.

THE SLAPSHIELD SAGA

AN INVITATION BY NASA

The Man from NASA calls Laurus one day at his home in Kirkjubaejarklaustur. He explains that he has looked far and wide for a landscape that might simulate conditions on the moon. Yes, a trip to that silvery star is promised, a Cabriolet, a Skiff-Rover has been designed and built for the express purpose of sauntering around upon it. Yet nowhere to date has been found to test its worthiness. Laurus's farmland, it would appear, exactly mirrors the topographical and geological character of the lunar-scape, so the Man from NASA exhorts Laurus the Lucky to make his pastures available to him. Laurus tells the Man from NASA that he is busy with his lambs and that, in any event, the only way to cross the lava field is by fleet of foot, as neither hoof nor tyre is up to the task:

The Vínlan'auts head off
Unpractised
In the Art of Roving
The Vínlan'auts head off
To make their Mark On The Moon.

THE REAL ILLUSION

THE SAMURAI

The Samurai smiles at the camera, his thin, navy-blue kimono clinging to his body in the fierce and freezing blast. He is a World Weary Warrior and, in his right hand, he grips a video camera, his trophy. Slapshield approaches and asks him to pose for a photograph. There they stand, two statues made of flesh, rooted to the boiling earth of Iceland's bubble-scape. Slapshield carefully prepares to frame him forever, to immortalise his spirit through the photic process, before snapping the picture. The Samurai can be seen calling out to him in the howling wind. Alas, Slapshield cannot hear him, for his words are carried off, in another direction, towards a figure in the distance:
"Mister! Mister!
Can you hear me?
Mister! Mister!
You reft your rens cap on!"

THE SLAPSHIELD SAGA

THE QUESTIONNAIRE

The questionnaire, duplicated on cheap paper, is placed at the breakfast table of the Hotel Athelstan, right in front of the Travelling Party. Slapshield completes his form perfunctorily and hands it back to the English schoolgirl who hovers with her parents in the background. It seems it is all part of a project for some distant examination. Leon the Note-Maker furrows his brow and considers the questions carefully, while Tura the Life-Giver exchanges glances with Sharplens. What natural resources are most easily harnessed in the region? What percentage of the Sagas is history and what percentage legend? Describe, in no more than one word, the spirit of the Icelandic people.

THE REAL ILLUSION

GREENLAND

According to the Landnámabók, the Icelander Gunnbjorn Ulfsson chanced upon Greenland around the year 900. Eirik the Red landed in 981 or 982, staying for three years or so on the west coast and subsequently giving it its name. Eirik was a distinguished entrepreneur and there can be no doubt that he deliberately hoodwinked those Icelanders who joined a return expedition in 985 or 986. He contended that "people would be much more tempted to go there if it had an attractive name". And he was right. At that time, the weather was warmer than it is now, and the "Mini Ice Age", which would freeze the river Thames in the Sixteenth Century, was a long way off on the meteorological horizon. When it did finally come, life on Greenland would become all but impossible.

THE SLAPSHIELD SAGA

GRAENLENDINGA SAGA

"I am not meant to discover more countries than this one we now live in," said Eirik. "This is as far as we go together." Eirik had just fallen from his horse and knew that it was a bad omen. So his eldest son, Leif, went on ahead without him and, in the course of time, discovered Vínland, or America, predating Columbus by half a millennium. It is said that the Genoese upstart passed through Reykjavík twenty years prior to his own Atlantic crossing in 1492. This may well have been the case, although some would claim it would have been easier to have gone directly from Iceland, following in the slippery path of the Vikings. Perhaps he had to go back to Portugal and Spain to find sponsors. Who knows? I like to think of Columbus in Reykjavík, marvelling at the light and at the lava-filled landscape, staring at the thin and towering beauties as they head towards his round and marbled café table.

THE REAL ILLUSION

THE ICELANDIC MODEL

When I open the door of Room 26 of the Hotel Thorg, I come face to face with the Icelandic Model, an elusive beauty with hair falling in a cascade to her slender hips. Setting aside my Toblerone wrappers, one of which is now covered with the opening words of my saga, I invite her to sit down and relax until Sharplens appears. Then I resume my work, removing the wrapper from another Toblerone and flattening it out carefully on the desk. "What are you doing?" enquires the Icelandic Model politely. This is the first time I have been asked what I am doing since landing on Iceland's shores. "I'm preparing my writing materials prior to setting down the next chapter of the Slapshield Saga," I reply. "The Slapshield Saga?" whispers the Flared One. "Is that the Missing Saga they told us about at school?"

"Maybe it is
Maybe it isn't
I suppose
It's a little too early to say."

THE SLAPSHIELD SAGA

THE ICELANDIC ARTIST

The Icelandic artist wears the captain's hat. His uniform is idiosyncratic, yet he wears it with pride and rarely leaves his post. An octogenarian, he is a study in befuddled aestheticism. His exhibition, above the café, consists of a series of sidelong glances at his native Icescape; the style is "naïve" at first but, upon closer inspection, becomes far more interesting. Slapshield encounters him in the gallery after enjoying a cursory luncheon and a glass of wine. The artist accosts him and talks lucidly about his work for some time, although Slapshield, not speaking the language, can only nod, sympathetically, in agreement. Later, they are reunited in the downstairs urinal, two strangers chatting contentedly in different tongues without comprehending a word of what the other is saying:

There they stand
The Artist as Poet
The Poet as Critic
Leaning with their Flies
Open in Iceland.

THE REAL ILLUSION

PLEASE TRY LATER

From his seat in the prow of the Red Skiff, Eirikur the Eagle-Beaked took up the telephone in his strong, bony hand. "All lines are busy," said a voice. "Please try later." Slapshield leaned forwards and tapped Eirikur on the shoulder. "Whose is that voice?" he enquired, discreetly. "It's the Telephone Girl," Eirikur replied. "I was in love with her once. And now, every time I call, she answers in the negative. There is no Viking this side of Friesland who has not heard her calling to them plaintively through the void. As for me, I once loved her and held her hand. Now I know she will never stop talking into my ear, as long as I live and breathe... and make telephone calls."

THE SLAPSHIELD SAGA

THE GREAT GLACIER

The glacier is history catching up with itself. It carves and sculpts the landscape right in front of Slapshield's eyes, so that he might enjoy its handiwork. Slapshield tends to view his surroundings as permanent; they constitute for him security, solidity, a helpful mass, a foothold. To find that geology is not archaic but a living science alters his perception of his surroundings, tangling the lines so thoughtfully drawn up for the purpose of customs, vacations and wars. The glacier is also a monster, its icy finger in every pocket, a vast, sluggish mass of white and grey ice stretching from the mountains to the sky, robbing Slapshield of a horizon against which to safely judge distance. Circumventing it for a few days, catching glimpses of its rounded, intrusive presence, he eventually ascends in order to inspect its scalloped features, feel its skin, dance about on its weakly powdered surfaces.

THE REAL ILLUSION

HIGH WALKERS

The twin-rounded hills appear on the horizon, identical, aloof in the mist. They are called the "high walkers". Mile after mile they punctuate the view that appears in the rear window of the Red Skiff. Later, snow bunkers dot the hill ridge, seemingly in negative, as if they were holes, poorly drawn, in the landscape. What is beyond remains a mystery, it is a void, a dimly encircled aperture through which only the imagination can travel. Slapshield lowers one eyelid, then another. He feels himself pulled through the safety screen beside him, so that he can no longer tell whether he is inside or outside the Skiff. And when he closes both eyes, simultaneously, tightly, all he can see are the twin hills rising ominously beyond the limits of his inscape.

THE SLAPSHIELD SAGA

THE PERMANENCE OF ICELAND

There are no monuments, no colonial houses, no great palaces with mirrors lining their innards, no powdered faces, big wigs or loose curls reflected vainly along their shiny surfaces. The Viking Empire was biodegradable and all the Eco and Ecco Maniacs applaud the sensitivity of its denizens towards the landscape. Like the Skraelings, the Vikings left precious few indicators of their passing: a small pile of rocks on a hill-top, rounded, eroded with grief; the amphitheatre, made by nature, called the Althing; and one or two hot-dog stops on the roadside. It is only the sagas that remain and they are the greatest *memento mori* of all:
They quietly fill
Farmhouse shelves
Link the Ages
And enchant
Visitors from abroad.

THE REAL ILLUSION

THE BROTHER OF LAURUS

The brother of Laurus the Lofty speaks little English and we speak no Norse. He is a stocky, strong and well-built man with piercing eyes and a way of walking which is so purposeful one has a job to imagine him doing anything else. For the first twenty-four hours, he does not smile. The Foursome accompany him, the next morning, travelling to an old farmhouse, which he and his brothers use for overnight stays when rounding up their sheep. From an inner pocket he produces a silver hip-flask and is soon pouring out measures of strong, transparent liquor. Using Slapshield's Sword Stick, he then cuts some portions of smoked lamb from a smouldering leg-let. "The horses sleep underneath us, in the barn. They keep us warm in the winter," he says, gruffly, as if repeating himself.

THE SLAPSHIELD SAGA

THE SCENE OF BATTLE

The profiles of fallen heroes are to be seen, staring out across the uneven valley. The battlefield is nearby and Slapshield can hear the cries of men as they charge forwards at one another, sword in hand. A small pile of rocks marks the place where Slapshield's ancestor, Stout Nose, fell, defending the honour of his family against a local farmer called Pinch-Hitter. It was a Pyrrhic victory: having sliced off Pinch-Hitter's legs with one swipe of his halberd, Stout Nose succumbed to his wounds and "the life ebbed from him like a glacial stream". Of the others who fell that day, their faces, carved in the basalt, can be glimpsed through the port windows of the Red Skiff as Eirikur steers it through a fjord. These men have stood vigil through the passing centuries and even now they await revenge in the thin, wet light.

THE REAL ILLUSION

SOME RUNES

Late in Egil's Saga, the eponymous hero cures a farmer's daughter of a grave malady. Every attempt, it seems, has been made to save her, to no avail; a local lad is commissioned to carve some runes for her, but this only worsens her condition. Egil is staying at the farmer's house and comments on the condition of the poor girl. He asks for her to be lifted out of bed and for clean sheets to be provided. Then he examines the bed and finds a whalebone with some runes carved upon it hidden in the mattress. After inspecting the runes, he scrapes them off and throws the bone into the fire. Then he places some fresh runes under the girl's pillow. Suddenly, she feels better. A few chapters later, the reader learns that she was the object of a great passion, that her suitor had been refused her hand by her father and, in desperation, had tried to seduce her by carving love-runes, "…but didn't have the skill". Yes, it was those runes that made her sick. "A mystery mistaken," chants Egil, sagaciously, "can bring men to misery."

THE SLAPSHIELD SAGA

IRISH MONKS

It is said that the first inhabitants of Iceland were Irish monks. One of them, whose name is a mystery, built the farm at Kirkjubaejarklaustur where Slapshield and his companions stay the night after a day's touring in the Red Skiff. This monk vowed that, after his passing, any non-believer who owned it would surely die. One day, a man of shaky faith approached his new property, the apocryphal farm. It seems he fell from his horse, stone dead, before even reaching the gate. According to Laurus the Leg-Puller.

THE REAL ILLUSION

THE STRANGEST OF BIRDS

The strangest of birds could well be an invention. There is a name for the genus, as you might expect, but Slapshield has a terrible memory for names. Early one morning, he stares at the bird with no name as it nose-dives straight for him, making a curious buzzing sound as it does so. It is a sound that is a cross between a click and a tock, suggesting, perhaps, that it is clockwork. Slapshield considers the nature of the bird. Is it malevolent? Is it an unhappy spirit? Does it have suicidal tendencies? Is it, finally, the kind of bird that one would wish one's daughter to marry, assuming one were a bird? Slapshield steps one or two paces forwards and the bird passes within an inch of his nose. He draws the catapult function from his Sword Stick and downs it using a pebble he keeps in his pocket. Then he walks over to where the bird fell. He turns it over onto its back; but he fails to locate the key. "As I thought!" he mutters, bumbling across the lava and sticking the bird under his helmet for safekeeping.

THE SLAPSHIELD SAGA

THE BIGGEST ERUPTION

In 1783, there was the Biggest Eruption. They found bits of it in China. The lava field stretched for mile upon mile and the whole of Iceland shook and trembled for a year. At the church of Kirkjubaejarklaustur, the vicar appealed to God to stop the lava from destroying the village, for it was fast approaching the church door. They say it was a miracle, but the lava did stop, right at the lych-gate:

> I stopped the Lava
> By crying "Our Father!"
> I stopped the Lava
> By calling forth
> A Medley of Discreet
> And Commendable Incantations.

THE REAL ILLUSION

THE IN-FLIGHT MAGAZINE

The Head Chef for Icelandair is called Jón Sigurdsson. He is managing director of the Keflavík Flight Kitchen. According to the In-Flight Magazine, he produces seven hundred and twenty thousand in-flight meals annually. His clientele also consumes over three hundred and seventy-four thousand miniatures, which are the small bottles one can also find in the Hotel Refrigerator of the Hotel Thorg. I now remove the last Four Roses and drink it in one, preparing myself for the voyage ahead.

THE SLAPSHIELD SAGA

EIRIKUR'S QUEST - PART TWO

Eirikur's dream to traverse Greenland's glacier remains intact: he is often seen weighing up the possibilities and the impossibilities as he steers the Red Skiff through the Wheelderness, stopping once in a while to check the tyre pressure or shift from two- to four-wheel drive. At such times, Slapshield can see him looking out, in the direction of the Great White Light, or Upwards to the Low Icelandic Heavens:
His phone unplugged
His eyes unpeeled
Through the Windshield!
Onward to the Hither-Beyond!

THE REAL ILLUSION

THE SHAPE CHANGER

"Onund was a tall man and stronger than anyone in the district. People were in two minds about whether or not he was a shape changer." Mention is often made in Egil's Saga of "shape changing", but no one can say exactly what a "shape changer" is. One day, Slapshield decides to change the shape of Iceland. First, he closes his eyes. Then he opens them again. Then he half closes them. Then he opens one eye and closes the other. Then he closes both eyes for an indefinite period. Things are going well but, upon repeating the process, he stumbles on the lip of a lava cave and disappears down a Devil's Hole. We next see him in a gay bar in downtown Sydney, fighting his way to the door with the aid of his Swiss Swivel Stick.

THE SLAPSHIELD SAGA

THE LAVA COURSE

Slapshield awakens in the night and looks through the window, across the Lava-Field-cum-Golf-Course. The house is built of the finest materials, but in miniature, as if for a child. Slapshield steps over the threshold, bumping his helmet on the lintel, heads out into Iceland and extracts a five-iron from his Sword Stick. In no time at all he has completed the course with a score of one under par. Then he returns to the house and goes back to bed. "Where have you been, Slapshield?" asks Sharplens. "I think I'm beginning to get the hang of this shape-changing business," he answers, unbuttoning his tunic and turning back to his dreams.

THE REAL ILLUSION

THE NEXT DAY

The next day never comes. Nevertheless, on the morrow, Slapshield picks up his helmet and sets off with Leon the Lyricker, to take vengeance against all the Wrongdoers of Historiography. Their first encounter is with the malevolent Freydis, whose atrocities in Vínland, recorded in the Graenlendinga Saga, are legion. Slapshield steps forward to summarily dispatch her, but Leon brushes his companion aside. "Let me deal with her!" he exclaims, removing his helmet and beginning to vibrate its multifarious tuning forks. "This helmet was made for me by James Hoarse Brush and it will play all the music I want it to, good or bad." And it is true for, within the space of three or four wags of a lamb's tail, Freydis is writhing about on the field, her hands to her ears, pleading with Leon to put his helmet back on his head. "Very well, Freydis," announces Leon. "But try getting on with people in future, instead of cutting off their heads and making a mischief of yourself!"

THE SLAPSHIELD SAGA

THE WEATHERMAN

They stare at the Weatherman one night as he gesticulates in a corner of the room. He is the brother of a friend, the Viking Artist, our Host in Absentia. His arms move in circles as he surveys the pockmarked map of Iceland, covered in arrows of wind inclined to every compass point. He is the Maker of Fire and Ice, the Man with the Plan, and all the world watches as he weaves his Mysteries:
> It will rain tomorrow
> It will not rain
> It will erupt tomorrow
> It will not erupt

Generally speaking, we can expect a partly cloudy, partly sunny day.

THE REAL ILLUSION

EXCALIBUR

    Slapshield bends down into the black sand in order to examine the Sword embedded in the scalloped dunes. It is impossible for him to open the blade, for the corrosion of countless tides has eroded and fossilised it almost to extinction. Noticing its axe/manicure implement, he realises that it must be the same weapon used by Egil Skallagrimsson, his ancestor, to murder Grim Helgason. Using his own sword stick, he carves a hole for it in a nearby cliff and gives it a decent, military burial:

The bad Workman
Blames his Tools
The Killer/Poet
Needs the right Implement.

THE SLAPSHIELD SAGA

THE GLACIAL LAKE

I have nearly reached the end of my saga. My stay is over and today I must quit my room at the Hotel Thorg. Checkout time is midday, but I have been offered a one-hour extension. In the bathroom, showering myself in the soft, blue Icelandic waters, I think of the fortnight I have spent on these craggy shores and of what I have achieved. I am pleased to have created Slapshield; I think we shall become good friends as time progresses, for everyone knows that friendship, unlike grief, requires time for sustenance. What strikes me most, above and beyond the vainglorious desire to capture the elusive colours and spectral forms of this ragged rascal of an island, is the poetry and grandeur of this place, inward and outward. Reaching within the Mini-Bar Refrigerator, I am astonished to find that there is not one miniature left. I peer inside, a little perplexed. It is then that I notice a small bundle of what I take at first to be chocolate bar wrappers, tucked away in a corner. All I can wonder now is who the chocolate thief might have been, unless it was Slapshield, of course, stealing treats in his sleep.

THE REAL ILLUSION

THE LAST PICTURE OF SLAPSHIELD

The Head, the Viking Helmet, Bandaged Balaclava, fashioned with great dexterity by the Buffalo-Dauber, Silk Skrínsson, juts out like a warning from the soft, grey mist of paint and sky. The blackened visor hides all, while the threads, neurological addenda, streaming nerve-ends, branch-lets, fibre-optics, knife-edged cord, fall away into the distance, making curious patterns in the glaciated back-scape. The Enemy, Black Rod, stands before him, a barrier, a post, erect, undiminished by his staring, resisting movement. This is the long-lost portrait of the warrior's innards, inverted, profiled, bisected, the Last Picture of Slapshield as he strides forth in order to provoke his Destiny:

The Unknown Soldier
Disappears forlorn
Into the Past
Into the Future
Towards a Battle Yet to be Named
By The Powers That Be.

THE SLAPSHIELD SAGA

PAINTED ROCKS

The rocks were painted by a little Icelandic girl.
Slapshield bought them from her for ten Krona the piece
After she had shown them to the Foursome at dinner.
Slapshield and the Nymph-Spirit then played Frisbee
Until the Sun didn't go Down.
As for the Rocks,
They now sit
Pride of Place
On a Desk In Vínland.

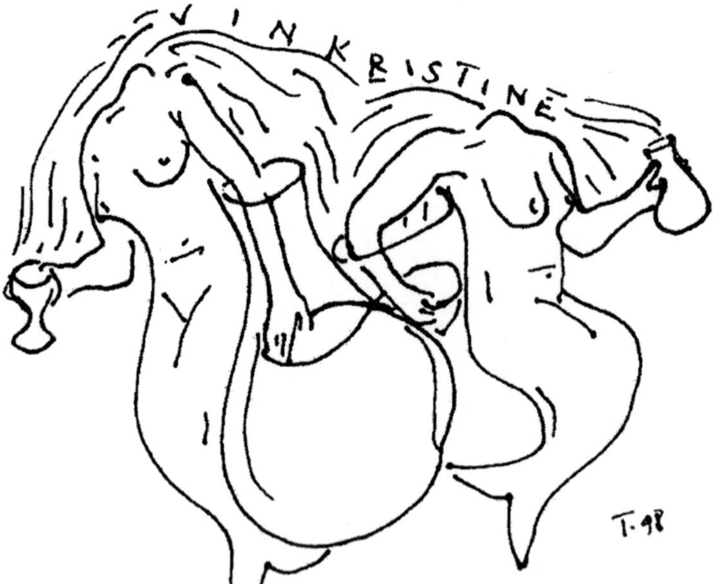
VIN KRISTINE
T. 98

THE VINKRISTINE SAGA
1998

There is no way forward. The idea is death. Love conquers all. Life is in the singular. I need to sleep now, Sea. Wake me up in an hour.

Voulez-vous vivre, Monsieur Lane?

I call her Sea, like the English C. I am pleased to have found her. She saved me. Pure and simple. Sea is not a writer but she knows how to work. The Saga is not literature; the form is oral, for now, at least. Who cares whether it's in French? I can always translate it into English later. I began by taping it on the small tape-recorder the other half gave me, but it is far easier to dictate to Sea, avoiding the laborious task of which I am currently incapable, of transcribing it onto paper. When I am well, I will rework it all anyway, turn it into a real Saga. Sea is a beauty, a Bretonne, doubtless of Celtic origin. She speaks not a word of English. She has green eyes, red hair. I have no idea when or how she appeared next to me. I awoke and there she was, in the cabin.

The drugs are out of date. So is the patient. And the hospital ship ploughs through the waves, trying to rid itself of all relevant metaphors, its great, rusting engines turning through the night. The captain is absent, the charts lie mildewed, illegible, and the crew, despite unquestionable loyalty, are only capable of taking care of themselves. Time passes, the ship crosses into the future and everyone prepares for the worst. Here, a storm is a trifle, a hurricane a diversion, yet the slightest technical concern, a modest change in speed or course confounds the entire company, for within this infernal, damp orbit, there can be no agreed proportion to tragedy.

The imagination can transport you left or right. In order to go straight on, to Oddlands, for example, you will need: the love of your nearest and dearest; an understanding of all side effects; an eclectic wardrobe.

The dawn repeats itself, surprising you. Grey shafts of light fall into the room and you welcome them warmly, as if the night you have just endured was death itself. What did the Specialist tell you? You were dying, Mr Lane. And now? What now? In one sense, you are as much dying as you are living and vice versa. You push death away, you think of it as the last line of your life, but in fact you carry it with you, it accompanies you on each page, either at the behest of Vinkristine or the Travelling Companion, within the theme of loss which never ceases to implicate itself in the story.

What is Oddlands? Oddlands is indispensable to the Vinkristine Saga, a place open to interpretation where the horizon is less of a line than a space. Oddlands is what you want it to be. It is not a dream. And, above all, not an idea. Oddlands can become your Garden of Eden, a faraway paradise in which reality and fiction conjoin. But, for me, Oddlands is a sacred spot, the place of my birth, the place of my death, as well as being the field of the last battle of the Vinkristine Saga. In that respect, it exists before and after time.

Yes, the Vinkristine Saga must include a battle because, if the Saga is a journey of some sort, it is also a struggle between death and the Treatment. Any love stories that punctuate the narrative must reflect this because love is a conflict of head and heart in its most extreme form. Not sure? You'll see soon enough.

THE VINKRISTINE SAGA

The Vinkristine Saga is an epic-in-progress whose goal is the salvation of the author, Simon Lane, alias Slapshield. It's not a joke. It's real. A question of life and death. The Saga must be dramatic without allowing anything to trivialise it. I have often been told I am a dramatic sort of person, but I am not at all. Life creates drama. And I play along with it, choosing the right part when it comes up. That's all.

There is no point in trying to understand everything. Ideas will not save you. When you fall into the deep you are not saved by an idea. You are saved by a lifebelt. The idea of dying dies as you dry yourself with a towel, looking at the sea as if it were an enemy you have fought and beaten.

Vinkristine makes my urine red. No. It's not Vinkristine. It's another *cellgift* whose name escapes me. I assumed it was Vinkristine but it's not. No matter. "Red?" asks the Specialist. "Yes, red." I am in the process of describing my condition as if I were another person. I am another person. It's obvious. Since the beginning, when I first ran into the Travelling Companion, I have become my own double. But isn't it something I should be used to by now? The writer and the invalid have a lot in common. I never thought I would use this illness as subject matter. But the opposite is the case: it's the illness that is using me. This doesn't really worry me, it's just part of the game we play together, the Travelling Companion and I. What bothers me is the red. If it isn't Vinkristine, then what is it? I should find out. Before I finish the Saga. I want everything to be just right. Am I speaking too quickly? Good.

And the Battle of Oddlands? It's a battle without a winner, in absolute terms. It's not a question of winning or losing, anyway. The two opposing sides may each gain a Pyrrhic victory, for example, or lose at the same time. Or the result could remain indecisive, balanced between the past (death-fear) and the future (life-in-hand). What is vital is reality; the facts. The presence of blood. There will inevitably be

THE REAL ILLUSION

numerous casualties. Even Vinkristine will be wounded, her left breast ripped by a needle-ticket. Vinkristine, you who are not red but, like each cured patient, possess true blood in your veins!

I stop for a moment. Vinkristine and the others have arrived and are now in position, suspended by the volumetric infusion pump. Vinkristine! I can't understand why at first I thought you were red. Must be your name. It turns out you are far from red, far from being any colour, in fact. You are more transparent than anything else, although you can become red according to the background; if, for example, there happens to be a bag of blood behind you. If there is one thing of which I am sure it is that you can only cure me by making me ill. Vinkristine! Fake goddess! Subtle monster! The woman I love, the woman I hate, the woman I love to hate! Boudicca killed sixty thousand Roman soldiers but she is an angel next to you. And herein lies the paradox: is it better to have Vinkristine with you or against you?

I awaken once again. The real struggle is with the imagination. Dreams are absurd, the only meaning they might have is in what they hide. I have become weak, empty. I am the contortionist who has forgotten how to fold his legs, a failed Houdini, a stage-struck Buster, a charmless Charlie. I have lost every possible attribute and I float on a sea of awful calm with not the slightest clue as to how to save myself.

The Battle of Oddlands will be the most epic scene ever put together in a medical feature. The entire cast of the Vinkristine Sage will appear, with thousands of extras, Travelling Companions, Contract-Nurses and Soldier-Models, along with all the key players: Slapshield, Moraes, Nimbus, Brayne, Helix and Helica, the Specialist, the Choreo-Scientist, the Dancer, Adriana, Phosphorcyclophemus and, of course, Vinkristine.

The Travelling Companion is your double, your partner, your

THE VINKRISTINE SAGA

sidekick during the Saga, right up to the decisive Battle of Oddlands. You can love him or loathe him, it doesn't matter, he is always at your side. The Travelling Companion is not the symbol of your illness. He is your illness. There are no symbols in the Saga. There are no ideas, either. Just real entities, like the Travelling Companion. If you can succeed in living with him you will keep yourself from falling in his shadow, because that is where death lurks.

And Onkovin? Another drug? Or another person? I don't know yet. But I like the name and I know that Onkovin already has a role to play in the Saga. He will fall in love with someone who will reject him cruelly. He will spend a great deal of time on his own. He will not know whether his destiny will be to save or to destroy the world. No one will be able to help him. No matter, he is taken from the pages of a real Icelandic Saga and is a true, inspiring player. He will eventually decide to save the world by joining the losing side in the Battle of Oddlands. Surrounded by wounded Contract-Nurses, he will raise the standard of battle to the epic-mythological. What do you think?

Before me stand the two thousand, three hundred and fifty models who want to become Model Soldiers. Why die, badly paid, in my Saga, when you can stay rich and alive as normal models? *Because we want to do something interesting!* they cry, in unison. I find it hard to choose between them so I take them all, dividing them into two groups: FRIEND and FOE. One model comes up to me with a seductive smile. "I want to be FOE." I decide immediately that she is the one who will play Vinkristine.

Our real lives pass by in our sleep, says Moraes de Tijuca, sculptor-in-residence of the Vinkristine Saga. Must be true, especially at dawn when I awaken or later, after a siesta, at that moment when my dreams still chase after me. The toxic infusion flushes through my veins after the initial skirmish with Vinkristine and the shock of this dreaded encounter rings in my ears as I turn my head to one side in an effort to understand my slumber, all the while trying to distance myself from the deepest fear imaginable that has overwhelmed me. Yes! I am still alive! Yes! Everything I do now is perfectly useless! The Saga will recommence as soon as I close my eyes again. Such is the power of the subconscious! I'll let it fight it all out for me; I have faith. It can win the battle for me. The battle is now as real as my sleep: it's true I am superfluous to events when I am awake. Moraes is right.

All illnesses are personifications. If they are born psychosomatically, they can die in the same way. They have their own lives, their problems, their doubts, their triumphs, their failures. They become a part of us in the way we become a part of them. They may become irritating, like dreams. If this happens, it's best not to talk about them unless you can find in them some universal element. Fear of death is universal, but this fear can be as close or as far as we can make it. The Vinkristine Saga is created so as to keep the Travelling Companion – and fear – at a secure distance equivalent to two breaking distance chevrons, as defined by the 1998 Highway Code.

Dying is an act rather than a state. But dying can in fact express both these things, because, if the act of dying itself is rather brisk, the state of dying can last days, months, a whole lifetime even. I find it much easier to accept the idea of *no longer being alive*. This is a state and never an act, one that describes death more precisely. A journalist in *Le Monde* wrote that when Eric Tabarly was lost overboard while caught in a storm near the Welsh coast he "stopped living" ("… *a cessé de vivre*"). Elsewhere in the article, he quotes the great yachtsman: "I often wonder how I will feel when I lose sight of land at the beginning of a crossing, but I have come to the conclusion I feel absolutely nothing whatsoever." Tabarly died because he wasn't using a safety harness. He found the idea repellent; so he died as a result of an idea. Tabarly's iconoclastic spirit is indispensable to my Saga and I am putting him in it right now.

THE VINKRISTINE SAGA

You no longer have any sense of normality. Whole months have passed since your first encounter with the Specialist. Numberless days and nights have made their mark on you forever. You are disorientated: Vinkristine, Steroids, Granocyte and Moscontin turn you upside down or from side to side without end; then you regain your equilibrium briefly without any chance of enjoying the moment before oscillating once again, around and around. You are not a victim, nor have you ever been one, you are just the product of a whole series of chemical reactions, one side of an equation in which x never attains a given value. The danger passes, you become abstract, the shadow of someone who was once you. The Saga has circumscribed your whole existence, yet you are reassured that everything is just a phase, even if you remain listless, without direction. Time passes. You open the window. You are no longer on board ship but in your favourite place, or spot. The clouds divide and the sun shines along summer pavements still wet with rain. You feel better. You turn to your lover. She wants to know how you are feeling. "Fine!" And, strangely enough, it's true, because you have not allowed the present – neither the illness nor the Treatment – to distract you.

The Battle of Oddlands is a test. Some people will say you are brave. But you are not. In one way, the presence of the Travelling Companion makes life, as well as death, easier to handle, for you do not have to do anything at all. It's just a question of obeying instructions. That is all. Is it bravery or obedience? If you do not complain, is it because you don't want to recognise your illness for what it is? You prefer to ignore it even if it controls your very existence. But is it actually true that it controls you? Or is it an illusion? Does it, perversely, make you special, interesting? The Battle of Oddlands will provide the answers.

You are in a strange place – Oddlands? – some foreign corner that may have been home once. You would rather not die there and you'd rather not live there either. You are stuck in the familiar aura of

THE REAL ILLUSION

childhood, surrounded by the necessary elements for survival: books, mineral water, postcards, a photograph of your other half. Oddlands is a place of childhood, foreign, yes, but one you have always loved, like the corner of rue de Buci and the rue de Seine, or a dirt road that runs to a farm in Tuscany along which you once walked, a long time ago, but which remains as familiar as the face that now appears in the doorway of your room.

The Specialist is worried about your behaviour. Apparently, you are acting strangely. He wants to send you to a psychiatrist. He has already made an appointment. "No," you exclaim. "It's not the inside that's the problem. It's the outside. The pieces don't fit together properly so what we need is an artist to redo the picture. The artist is nature, the image is my world. Apart from that there is no solution. Because there is no problem. The thoughts of Wittgenstein, the abstractions of Turner and the complete works of Laurence Sterne are what is needed here. But a psychiatrist? Renting an ear is the first sign of madness.

You were dying!

The double helix of DNA (perfect embrace, acme of desire) divides and one part, Helica, manages to pierce the membrane of the target-cell in a dance created by the Choreo-Scientist. This story constitutes an epic theme in the Saga, a real love story in which Helix and Helica become separated in heroic circumstances and spend the duration of the Saga trying to find one another again.

The illness is a malediction, the cure, a benediction. Good and evil shake hands before and after the battle. White cells are dispersed by a strike of Vinkristine, the nervous system short-circuits during the bombardment and the *corpus intactum* – that's you – becomes both actor and spectator simultaneously for the duration of the conflict. There are no knights, no soldiers, no heroes, just a horde of Contract-

THE VINKRISTINE SAGA

Nurses clamping your feet to the bed and calling for assistance to move you onto another floor.

No. You are not a rat. And science is not the cure. Science is an old gentleman with kind eyes who talks sweetly in front of the camera. "People often ask me when I will retire. I tell them one day I will return to the ease of childhood." The old man is in his laboratory somewhere in America, speaking of his Grail, the cure he has invented for the disease that will never be used because of the side effects. While he talks, I realise he has become a character in the Vinkristine Saga. He is a warrior, a veteran, the microscope is his sword, the double helix of DNA his shield. If my illness is childhood, then this scientist is my father, working modestly in his laboratory while I sleep across the ocean, his work leading directly to cabin No. 202. "It's like trying to get across the Rockies. You reach an impasse. So you find another way."

And Helix? Still separated from his lover, he spends his time looking for any clues to Helica's movements, a whiff of her perfume perhaps, or her sweat, for that matter. Anything at all. Meanwhile, Helica is doing what she can to make me better, attaching herself tirelessly to cell-targets: she is just too far away from him. In desperation, Helix travels to every corner of the world, his heart hollowed by anxiety, seeking acts of heroism he thinks might appease the gods.

Fear is an illusion. What provokes it may be very real but that has nothing to do with fear itself. Fear claims to be in control but anything uncontrollable can become controllable, just as all things may invite their own antithesis. Love can be transformed into hate with a phrase, an inflection, while fear can turn to euphoria long before the Titanic has made a hole in the cinema floor. Whether or not certain things can be controlled, we are always subject to the capricious side of nature which, with stunning perversity, turns death into a joke as Poo, the Malaysian Contract-Nurse, carries another vase of flowers into the

THE REAL ILLUSION

cabin, transforming it briefly into a funeral parlour.

You were dying!

To live with your illness, the Travelling Companion, that is, you will need a doctor and a Specialist. But you will also need a sense of humour. Without these elements you will fail. You will always have your Travelling Companion, of course, but it is more than likely he won't be the kind you like. Whatever the case, you will regard him with affection and derision in equal quantities. Affection? Of course, because the Travelling Companion is a part of you and you see in his shadow your own reflection.

I see in my Travelling Companion the stigmata of an errant existence that I have loved in all its most absurd and poignant details. My Travelling Companion and I are friends and I aim to kill him with kindness. If my Travelling Companion kills me first, it is obvious he will also be killing himself, so wherever I happen to be, or not to be, my laughter will resonate in the ears of the quick, as both tribute and curse.

The Celebrity-Nurse is filling me up with Vinkristine. She takes the bazooka and sticks it into the canula attached to my forearm. I stay perfectly still on my bed, feeling the first wave of heat enter my body, staring up at the infusion pump for a moment. Now it is Adriana's turn. The wave becomes hotter. It is now, finally, I realise that Adriana is the red one! Adriana! *La Rossa!*

Time passes across the pages of an empty diary. The numbered days seem more arbitrary than ever, their only use being to mark the endlessly repeated intervals in the Treatment, by visits to hospital and meetings with Vinkristine, Adriana and Onkovin. You have become a mixture of side effects, an oral pain-poem, a Saga whose author remains a mystery. You wake up at three in the morning, at three in the afternoon, you stare up at the ceiling of your room, you read, you talk, you listen, you recall other Sagas, other protagonists you have created; who have also created you.

Do you want to live?

When I met the Travelling Companion for the first time, I knew he could kill me. He still can. But now there is a difference: I can kill him too. I could have killed him from the beginning, but I am only beginning to realise that I am capable of doing to him what he has always been capable of doing to me. But when can it have been that I crossed that line, if that line ever really existed? At the beginning, I was very weak, incapable of doing anything, but I could, theoretically, have accomplished what my physical incapacity prevented me from doing by using my intuitive powers, even though they were also weakened. But what of that imaginary line? I think it must have appeared at the very moment I decided to write the Saga, when I began dictating it to Sea. There is no way forward. The idea is death.

As for the Travelling Companion, he seems to have disappeared. Vanished. He can still kill me. He could die peacefully, like an old friend, tired of life. The Vinkristine Saga is full of paradoxes. The very nature of the Travelling Companion is a prime example. The ultimate enemy is also an old friend, a killer who can disappear with all the politeness and discretion of a diplomat. He is a poison that is also a stimulant for existence. The Travelling Companion seeks death, while I seek life, but these two brutal, unequivocal facts conceal a subtle relationship. Each of us counts on the other, each is at either end of a scale on which the point of equilibrium is the imagination.

Give me a rat and I'll find a cure!

People like to think the body and the soul are separate entities. This idea has a great deal to do with the fact that we consider ourselves superior beings. In fact, our needs and instincts are fairly basic for the most part, and our desires very simple. Even a great philosopher likes a little comfort, food and sex. As soon as we realise we are just one entity our attitude changes. Shakespeare knew about such matters. If music be the food of love. Everything is mixed up. Nothing is divisible. Nothing is explicable. Ideas are dangerous. All generalisations are false. Language is an approximation. Love conquers all. The cure lies within the problem. So there you have it, in a nutshell!

Now that we can consider the Travelling Companion as an intruder in the body-soul mechanism, we can go about making an amicable settlement in order to become whole. The result? Our desires and our thoughts now blend naturally, leaving but a shadow of a question mark on our forehead.

Moraes and his wife have sent me some *babosa* by Federal Express from Rio. I read out the recipe to Alex, my editor, who cuts the leaves of the plant before mixing them with honey and *cachaça*. Vinkristine, Adriana (*la Rossa*), Onkovin and the others are all jealous of the *babosa* because *babosa* is pure and uncomplicated. *Babosa* comes from nature, not from a laboratory. *Babosa* doesn't pretend to be anything other than it is. It promises nothing. It gives no side effects, other than inebriation of health. *Babosa* and Slapshield embrace one another and Sea looks on with a smile. Do you want to live? Do you want to be saved? By love? By a Brazilian cactus?

Equilibrium is the thing. It has to be maintained. Equilibrium is a very personal and mysterious business, incomprehensible to others. Even the Choreo-Scientist doesn't understand it. Everyone is capable of understanding his own equilibrium. But to maintain it requires action. The Battle of Oddlands is a means of creating equilibrium. But there are more subtle ways of going about it. Writing is one. Drinking *cachaça*. Making love. Avoiding oysters in May. You create rules so you can break them. What remains becomes your personal philosophy of equilibrium.

Beyond: the horizon. Further still: Oddlands. Oddlands, the beginning and the end of a vicious circle. I step back. It's not time yet. I rest my head on the pillow, I close my eyes, ridding my mind of the image with a sweep of my arm and sending it towards the window. I halt time as time halts me. And I wait. If I awaken, I am not dead. If I am not dead, I will awaken. Science has now become too complicated for me. I am reduced to the simplest possible idea: I am alive.

A trail of smoke in the sky, an arrow showing an unknown tangent, a line disappearing from a picture in blue. Beyond the line – before and after it – infinity is revealed by default; the white trail of smoke grows thicker in close-up before growing invisible once again, as if it had never existed. Yes, eternity, the backdrop for everything that might happen, or might never happen!

The sunset is pink, a brush of *la Rossa* Adriana diluted in water. Everything becomes blurred, the view through the porthole is no more than a compromise offered up to me by nature to give me comfort. But it doesn't comfort me, that's the point. I take a dose of pills and I think of Helix, crossing another mountain or a wave of ice. His odyssey, like mine, seems to be progressing, but it remains a journey without end, as if we had become two minuscule specimens under our creator's microscope. While Helix uses love to advance, I use pain, anguish and fear. Positive, negative, each element becomes equal, the emotions that drive us losing their true meaning, judged simply by their usefulness. Love and fear, for example, end up having the same value; and Helix and I become controlled more by their effects than by their substance. Everything is as blurred as the sky. And I turn my head away again to avoid it.

THE REAL ILLUSION

The night extends to infinity. One huge cloud – grey and deep – fills that part of sky that falls to the sea. Stars appear above my head, too far away for me to distinguish them properly. Everything is an illusion, near or far, a trick created at my expense to keep my dreams away from danger and abstract me from a world that is both mine and alien to me. Yes, I am my world. But what is this world, of what might it consist? The ship is behind me, the sea leads me to a placed filled with negation and I am just here, alone, bereft. My closest friends – Moraes, Brayne, Helix and the others – have disappeared behind the curtain that is night, there is nothing and nobody to hide me and I am exposed as never before to this picture in four dimensions. Time will move forwards, the dawn will come to rescue me but for now the night will continue to hurt for as long as it lasts.

The night! True damnation! The death of all and everything. Sea! Where are you? I listen to my voice on the tape-recorder as if each sentence is my last. "Action is character," said F. Scott Fitzgerald. He was right. Henceforth, only acts will define my characters, only action will lead me and my cast to that sacred meeting point: Oddlands!

THE DEVIL AIN'T BAD, EITHER
2001

I am supposed to be writing a book, but the book is writing me. The book is not "about" anything, it is just part of an autobiography which will only end when I do. I suppose in that sense it is "about" me, even if I am not always sure exactly who that person might be. I look into the bathroom mirror as I shave and I wonder at the inverted view it offers, the left hand usurping its counterpart in a lathery brush of cheek so that I not only seem foreign to myself but also ambidextrous. Meanwhile, the whole world turns and I turn with it, as we all do, subconsciously. Gravity is our refuge, we whose dreams march us through the night. It keeps us from falling, but not from falling in love.

I was in a film last week. A film director came down from New York. He is Argentine but he had clearly adopted the habits and disposition of the New Yorker. People from New York always seem rather out of place here in Rio de Janeiro. They arrive with ideas and they sweat in the heat and in the pursuit of their ambition. This man was fairly typical. I had to play the part of a magician and I improvised, shuffling a pack of cards and thinking of what Buster Keaton would have done. I wanted to imitate that blank stare of Buster's as he puts his hand to his forehead and looks into the distance. When I saw the rushes I realised I had only partially succeeded. But what is success, anyway? I am not here to succeed, I am here to restore myself to an original idea and write something that sounds good.

THE REAL ILLUSION

When I was young, I thought life was easy. I was right. It's a piece of cake. Soon to be forty-four years old, I have seen sadness, I have flirted with death, I have buried friends and I have watched my heart break, like an old clock. And what of it? The past disappears through that haze stretching from the horizon, the sound of the sea slips between my ears like a blessing, the shadow of a small cloud caught by the sun stands between me and what will happen next. One loses oneself within the moment, one holds onto it, one doesn't let go, and, if the moment is good, as moments tend to be in this place, it will lead to whatever happens to work best.

This place – Rio de Janeiro – is full of beauty. There are twice as many girls as boys and at least half the girls are beautiful, so the ratio of pretty girls to all boys is even. What else? People seem happy. I was at the airport the other day to pick up my daughter. It was seven in the morning. I saw three airport workers standing in the Arrivals area and laughing. I have no idea what had made them laugh, but that's what they were doing. Perhaps they were laughing because they had just read, as I had done, the new statistics on Rio, including the fact that girls outnumber boys by two to one. It doesn't really matter why they were laughing, what mattered was that the first thing my daughter heard upon arriving was laughter. I like that.

This is a good place to live and this is a good place to die. But I want George to be the barman at the wake. And no sandwiches. Just *caipirinhas* with *cachaça* (not vodka) and some steak, rice and salad. And some red wine. Chilean will do. I want my last meal after I am dead, for my friends, so I can look down, or up, or sideways, at the whole thing, even if one hand still doesn't know what the other hand is doing. If death is a ceremony, why shouldn't life be one too?

One night, I went into the *favela* with my friend, Tunga. It was late. We had been to a party and then we went into Rocinha to see what was happening. It was four in the morning and we found a bar and drank

THE DEVIL AIN'T BAD, EITHER

beer. Young men in shorts and t-shirts cradled AK-47s in their arms awaiting trouble and we stood at the counter of the bar in silence. "It's best not to look them in the eye," Tunga said. The barman stared at a television, watching one of those Hollywood films in which violence is like the sex in a pornographic film, used intermittently between boring sections of the story so as to keep people interested. Every time someone got shot or blown up, he burst out laughing. A man ran past me with a gun in his hand and I drank my beer without moving a muscle. I wasn't acting any more; I was being me for a change. It was a strange feeling.

It's true to say I don't do very much here at the moment. I watch and I listen and I live. It requires a certain pleasurable momentum to be at peace with oneself. It amuses me to see myself acting in a movie without end without ever having to write or learn the script. So many things happen which fit into the story, I can't quite believe it all, the timing is always perfect, the sensations always sublime. My dreams are dull and insignificant, they have no effect on me, they are scenes and pictures from the past that belong to a different person. As for Rio de Janeiro, I am convinced I could stay here forever. Someone last night asked me how long I plan on staying here. "I don't know," I replied. "Until I die." As for work, if I am to observe more than invent I'll just write down everything that's going around me and try to sell it as news.

No, the future and the past no longer exist and I bathe in a warm pool, which is the present. Nothing surprises me, I have become entirely open to circumstance and I allow nothing to impede my happiness. I just stepped outside and I looked down at the sea, the great South Atlantic. A container ship was heading south at speed and, nearer to the shore, a fishing vessel was hove to in the swell. Then I came back to my room to write this down. It occurs to me, as I do so, that time really is an illusion, which is the real reason why I cannot say how long I will be here. Time is not in my hands. Because it doesn't really exist. Leave immortality to the gods, they can afford it.

THE REAL ILLUSION

During *Carnaval* I was invited to take part in the *desfila*. I was cast as a devil and a costume was provided for me. I stood at the bar all night making jokes with a French diplomat and I couldn't find my costume when the time came to join the parade. It was seven in the morning as "Grande Rio" prepared to go on. Still without costume, I was taken away from the devil section and pushed into another, in which everyone was dressed as beggars, but another marshal told me I looked too scruffy and kicked me out of the parade. I went back to the bar and had a whisky. My new friend was very amusing. He wanted to give me a medal. "What for?" I asked. He is the most decent Frenchman I have met here. We talked about culture at one point and I said I don't think it exists – just as I don't think time exists – unless it means a lot of individuals doing different things in the same place and getting medals for it.

What do culture and knowledge and theories all add up to? People have got the wrong idea about this place. In Europe, Brazil is considered a "developing" country, but what does that mean? I consider Brazil to be very civilised because I think the people are very civilised. They are funny and quick-witted and they know what life is. And me? How do I fit in? I belong to no culture, I am just a writer who was born in England and who now lives in Rio de Janeiro. No one has ever heard of me, I am invisible to the world and that is the way I like it. When I was in London a few months ago, a friend told me I was a "wasted talent", which I took as a compliment. Better wasted than none at all. As for being talked about or written about, what difference does that make? Just don't believe everything you read in the papers.

WHEN THE COLONEL DIES, CHRIST WILL DISAPPEAR FOREVER
2000

When the Colonel dies, Christ will disappear forever. The Englishman opposite will long since have returned home. I will no longer see him and hear him drinking himself to oblivion on the terrace of his apartment opposite. I will no longer catch his inflated face in the "Paz e Amor", trembling hand grasping his gin and tonic, nervous laughter and flickering eye registering the sniff of one of a thousand lines of cheap, crumbling coke; I will no longer see him stare vainly across the table to his imperious *mulatta*, of whom he is so clearly proud. Sometimes, I see her glide across the floor of his living room or stand in front of the mirror, combing her thick, black locks. He could have done better, he could have done worse, I cannot decide whether she was once a hooker; it's hard to tell. The day will come, as it always does, when they will find themselves at the airport, one of a myriad of couples lost in some desolate embrace, a tear will fall onto the polished marble, he will be gone and Rio will be a memory to be kept for old age.

When the Colonel dies, Christ will disappear forever. They have offered him a fortune but he stays on, relic of a former age in which Rio was made up of villas. This last villa in the street will fall to dust and a tall apartment building will take its place, blocking Christ the Redeemer from view. For now, I can see the great statue half shrouded in cloud, or mist, or both. There it stands, encased in scaffolding, for even Our Saviour needs renovating occasionally. And below, the still, flat lake, starved of oxygen, reaps its daily harvest of dead fish, rising to the surface and floating uselessly to the far shore. Sculls and eights

THE REAL ILLUSION

often appear, slicing the water and disappearing behind the apartment building to the left of the Colonel's house. There is something English about the scene, wholly contrasted by the thick, tropical air and sunlight breaking through the cloud.

For how long have I stared through this window at the view? How many times have I been rescued by its beauty, its completeness, its sumptuous reflection? Yesterday, I watched the dawn appear, strands of cloud coloured blue and pink, the waters of the Lagoa as flat and as still as never before, I felt the light strengthen and the air change into a dewy, humid embrace. Looking down at the cobbled sidewalk, looking up towards the Redeemer, looking over to the terrace doors of the apartment, closed for sleep and the inevitable hangover. Today is no different.

Soon, I will step out and walk down the street, turning a corner into rua Garcia d'Avila. It is mid-afternoon, the regulars crowd the bar, cold beer in hand, the tables are full with families, children, waiters shouting orders to the counter. I will take my place to buy some cigarettes and then walk on to the café on Visconde de Pirajá, buy a *pão doce* and drink a coffee. The short, wiry shop assistant will be attending to the roast chickens, drawing them from a spit and dumping them into a tray. A *mulatta* with impossibly tight jeans and thick, bulbous thighs will pass by, then an old man, possibly European, walking shakily with a stick, some boys will appear from the beach and loiter beside me, chatting and laughing, and I will simply stand and watch and listen, the coffee seeping into my nervous system, accelerating my thoughts.

I will walk around the block, stop at the newsstand, buy the paper and return to the "Paz e Amor" for a beer and a bowl of soup. I have not gone to the beach; I rarely go, although when I do I always enjoy the lazily defined pointlessness of it, the surf, the South Atlantic racing to the shore from some distant horizon half-blurred by spray, the heat, even the sand, the sight and sound of Cariocas lying around or standing, cigarettes in hand, glancing down at their deepening suntans or perhaps striding confidently to the shore and diving into the fierce, seductive foam. "*O mar, misterioso mar/Que vem do horizonte!*"

WHEN THE COLONEL DIES, CHRIST WILL DISAPPEAR FOREVER

And then? Then I will return to my place, to my view, to the familiarity, which never quite loses its freshness. Little will have changed, the cloud might have thickened and Christ might have disappeared for a moment. But, of course, when the Colonel dies, Christ will disappear forever.

BETWEEN GEOGRAPHY AND SCIENCE
1985

Allow me to introduce myself. My name is Sand Dollar. I was born at a time only myself and members of the geological fraternity would call "comparatively recently". This was before our great continents parted, when Britannia was but a twinkle in God's eye, when all the world was known as Pangaea and when the shape of the land masses, which now fill the pages of your atlas, was nothing but a scribbled plan on a rock.

At that time, God was planning things for your future, in much the same way as He does now. How hard it is to conceive of the impermanence of your surroundings when your surroundings are all you have at your disposal; how hard it is for you to imagine, say, the East End of London bordering on the Maldive Islands. But this you must do in order to conceive of such a strange state of affairs.

Yes, long ago and no mistake. I remember, one hazy afternoon, seeing God bending over an imposing lump of sandstone, scratching His head with His finger, just as Stan Laurel would do so many millions of years later. Actually, He looked rather like Stan Laurel, except for the fact that He was almost completely bald. He had heard me crawling up behind Him and had turned to see what was going on. I suppose I had quite unnerved Him; He was human, after all. Some people, especially the *Zhding*, or Highland People, said that He had been sent down from above, that He was actually the Son of God and that He had been charged with saving man's soul. Others subscribed to the view that although He was, indeed, the son of God, His real task was not to save man's soul but simply to supervise the parting of the great continents,

THE REAL ILLUSION

evidently in the hope that, by so doing, man would be able to save his own soul, there being considerable animosity around Pangaea as a result of a lack of space. Still others, notably the *Zhdnotta*, or Cynical Ones, maintained that He was not the Son of God at all but a jobbing architect by the name of God, short for "Godfrey".

I was undecided. Besides, I was too young to do anything but believe in the opinions expressed by the nearest and most frightening adult. All I knew was that God was someone very important and very different, not least because everything else in the world began with the letters *Zhd*. At a very early age I had leafed through the pages of our thirty-volume dictionary, gazing in wonderment at the single entry under the letter G.

God. (Origin unknown) God. Or Son of God. Or both. Architect?

To add to this uncertainty, I was also living in an environment in which time, as I have intimated, had little relevance. As I recall, it only really become popular later on, with the sundial manufacturers, the candle makers and the Swiss. To be honest, we felt no real need for it; we had the sun, the light and the darkness, and we ate when we were hungry. Food and water were plentiful, so there was no need for work or industry of any kind. I was the only one with any career objective, for I wished to record what was going on around me and write stories about it. I would spend hours writing on tablets, on animal tusks and on the walls of a cave situated near the *Zhding* settlement, often working until after twilight. As a result, I began to suffer from short-sightedness. Even our eyes were different then; they were more like shells, a fact that might possibly explain my name. Many people I knew didn't use their eyes at all, favouring their other senses. We were simple folk and not known for greediness. Nevertheless, my eyes were very important to me and it was with their weakening powers in mind that I summoned the courage to approach God that day.

"Bad eyes, eh?" said God, furrowing His brow and continuing to scratch His head.

"Yes, God. They seem to get weaker all the time," I replied, timorously.

BETWEEN GEOGRAPHY AND SCIENCE

"Are they important to you, Sand Dollar?"

"I beg Your pardon?" I asked, my voice wavering uncontrollably.

"Well, if your eyes are important to you, why do you maltreat them so, by working and writing on tablets, cave walls and animal tusks until after the sun has gone down?"

"They are important to me, God, for I have ambition and I work hard to fulfil my dreams."

"Ambition?" replied God, shaking His head. "I haven't heard of that for ages. Not since the Tree Planet." There was a pause. "So you have ambition and you wish to fulfil your dreams?"

"Yes, God."

"Very well, I will keep your eyes in perfect condition for you, I will give you immortality to give you the time to fulfil your dreams and I will give you the task of writing the story of your life. Now, leave me in peace. I have work to do."

"Thank you, God."

After that I was never in any doubt as to the power and wonder of God. I steered well clear of the *Zhdnotta*, or Cynical Ones, and I spent more and more time with the *Zhding*, or Highland People, recording what they had to say on tablets. Time, or its equivalent, passed and soon enough the great continents began to part. The salt water divided Pangaea, the *Zhdnotta*, thankfully, became isolated and moved East and the *Zhding*, to my consternation, moved West. As for me, I found myself on a small island, quite alone, moving in a north-westerly direction.

Unfortunately, much of my writing was not portable and I was only able to save two leaf-bags of animal-tusk books, along with the odd pile of stone tablets which was left on my island (these I would have published, much later, in an American scientific quarterly called *Recreationism*). As for the rest, I fear much of it was destroyed or, worse, plagiarised by unimaginative writers and religious fanatics. I can verify this for I happen to know for a fact that the singing monkey referred to in the writings of the Prophet Zin was not the latter's invention at all but actually something I had recorded some three million years earlier.

THE REAL ILLUSION

As my island moved across the oceans at an indiscernible speed, I began to grow restless and despondent. I tried to communicate with God in a variety of ways, including pretending He was not there in order that He might deign to prove that He was, but I met with little success. I did come across something one morning that reminded me of His continued interest in my welfare but this, like everything else at the time, had an aura of ambiguity about it. It was a pebble on the beach with the letter *G* scratched onto it. Far from consoling me, it actually had the opposite effect and I felt more lost than ever as a result of the sighting. I began to wonder what kind of a blessing immortality was in the face of such loneliness, in the absence of writing materials (as soon as I started a sentence I would have to search for another pebble, there being no fresh tablets, animal tusks or cave walls at my disposal), and in the lack of interesting subject matter available to me. I survived by keeping myself busy recording such things as tidal currents, wave heights and the movement of clouds, but more often than not I would find myself seated on the beach in a state of bewilderment, gazing into the distance with my perfect shell-eyes.

Then, one day, God appeared. "Sand Dollar! You look dejected! Have you no faith?"

"Yes, God, I have faith. But where am I going?"

"You are headed away from Pangaea. Be not afraid, for soon you will come to rest. Can you not feel the change in temperature?" And, with that, He was gone.

His appearance strengthened my resolve and rekindled my excitement about immortality. Sure enough, after a while, I had the unmistakable feeling that we had stopped moving. Henceforth, time began to take on meaning, which at first frightened me but which eventually placed me in some kind of historical context. It started to rain frequently and, as if that might in itself have imbued the atmosphere with fecundity, my island began to fill with people. My life took on a new perspective and I felt less anxious about my future, even though my new neighbours made me wonder whether I would not have been better off in Pangaea, for they were rough and aggressive and fiercely defensive of a land they saw as their own. I have no idea how they came to arrive on my island, save for the fact that some extraneous element, some part of another great continent, might have collided with my own, modest domain. They spoke a strange language which I learned only with difficulty, they grunted a lot and bred like rabbits and seemed to have no feeling whatsoever for the finer things in life. I studied their habits and wrote about them, making use of a new writing material called paper, made from trees. It took me a while to get used to but I found that with so many things changing around me I became more and more adaptable. One thing I could never get used to was the warfare. God, my oldest and greatest Friend, had taught me that life was sacred and I could never understand why these savage islanders could kill each without mercy. During a particularly long period of strife I considered the advantages of emigrating, a decision I ultimately postponed until what people now call 1979. This date fell in an era of uneasy peace known as the post-war or pre-war period and I often ask myself whether even my divinely gifted immortality would have saved me from the eventual carnage. I chose for my new home the Tree Planet, which suited me well for many years. Paper was plentiful there and people kept themselves to themselves. I am happy to say that, as a result, I never regretted the move.

THE FORECAST
2009

The conditions are middling to desperate.

A large depression is moving east from mid-Atlantic, joining another weather system which has, for some days now, obscured the land mass. The only parts currently visible to the camera are ill defined, illusory, for there is no coastline to assist the process of definition. Albion itself becomes an illusion, a piece of sustained guesswork, boldly indicated by the hand of the meteorologist, yet perfidious and elusive nonetheless, a contour, an outline, superimposed upon one vast cloud six thousand metres thick, stretching from Hastings to the Hebrides.

My own outline now appears upon the forecast, one arm stretching forwards to the Bar in an arc describing a broad swathe over the Peak District, another moving to a side pocket which is the Garden of England, bisecting the narrower, concentric lines of a cold front, yet another illusion, of course, for how can a line truly delineate anything at all, unless by default, a murdered profile on a sidewalk perhaps, yet hardly this, a man holding a glass the size of Ireland, or an entire kingdom, obscured by cloud? Extracting a Lucky Light and bringing it to tremulous lips, I watch in vain as the smoke rises so as to fill in the gaps, obliterating all and everything.

We, in this place, within the conditions laid out for us, move in time to the front, under the outline, under the cloud, under the weight of the Bar's mouldings. We are, all of us, ghosts, for, just as Albion itself

THE REAL ILLUSION

is an illusion, so too are its inhabitants, pushed here and there, bullied back and forth by the weather's errant rain, the weatherman's errant crayon, whose scratchings on our corporate destiny belittle us, making us wonder who might really be in charge, after all, if not God.

Down below, the city, a great dampen swirl in which figures, grotesque, contorted, appear within the rage of winter, fighting through the ink and cloud of a night first glimpsed from afar, in space, heads bent, eyes narrowed to the clock, awaiting first and last orders. The satellite turns in a slow spiral, relaying the conditions with impunity, performing its melancholy dance through the void. It cannot lie, it cannot tell us where we are truly headed. And its labour is a lament for all unsaid.

News just in! Ninety per cent chance of rain!

Naturally, we are not all of us ghosts. That would be to overstate the issue. Some of us rejoin the quick in order to make ourselves heard above the fearsome din of this place, barking an order to Frank or Mason through the smoke and cloud and chalk dust. Dead or alive, however, only those with an understanding of the conditions are served. And while there are often those present who are irrefutably dead and may well have been for some time, there is always a regular splattering of the forever-mortal, a young artist in flared trousers, perhaps, or an older one with no trousers at all.

"I am a…"

Perhaps *ghosts* is inappropriate, I am thinking more of spirits, ideas, projections, for everything and everyone is a projection of someone else, in accordance with the acknowledged egocentricity of the species and the spending power of the individual. As for the place, it too converts, inverts, perverts, those who move within it, engulfing them in the same pervasive cloud as it engineers the crimes for which it is celebrated.

THE FORECAST

And, as death becomes cheapened, so life becomes affordable only to those with the means, however criminal. The rules are a paradox, involuntary parking and manslaughter being wholly interchangeable, and all sentences remain suspended as the great drunken mass sinks into the shelf of Atlanticus.

"I am a drinker..."

Aside from the means and the conditions are the references, myriad, confused. Of note, the trivial, the literary and the aesthetic, for we exist, after all, in a climate not only of damp but also of *pastiche*. This is not to say we ourselves are insipid, it simply reflects the way in which we are projected in order to satisfy the exigencies of fashion, a repetitive, eclectic cycle of ideas which serves to revive interest in the primary condition: existence. Being both backward- and forward-looking, we are able, under the cloud, to defy not only space, but also time, so that the present can be anything we wish it to be. Only a few of us are party to the fact that 2008 is actually 1908, artists mostly, recreating a modernism which has yet to exist. Splendid conceit, worthy of prizes, medals even!

A wholly democratic institution, the Bar welcomes all comers, despite the avowedly strict policy instituted by the forefathers, a round table of eccentrics and deviants whose cigar smoke still clings tenaciously to the ceiling. If these most senior of spirits were truly dead, of course, they would turn in their graves. As it is, their coarse laughter and thigh-slapping will forever echo within the precincts of this monstrous edifice, true microcosm of a true, if elusive, sphere: London! City of Crime!

Amongst us, at any given time, are the uprights, punctuating the crowd, odd parenthesis to the suspended sentence, neat counterpoint to the inevitable huddle of impostors. One is always careful to avoid the latter, yet this is sometimes rendered impossible by a glimpse of a pert breast or a wistful smile, misguided lust blurring any critical abilities still extant after sustained intoxication. Yes, the saturation of all senses is one of the principal conditions, without which all others become void.

Not even I, part participant, am exempt. Only recently I found myself drawn to a woman of torrential beauty. Was she a ghost? I could not say. That she was actually a man only came to light when Mason, crossing the bar in order to silence an impostor with a nifty thwack of his Colin Cowdrey Special, turned to me confidentially:

I advise against it, sir. Unless that is your particular fancy, said he, wiping the blood from the bat's edge with a rag.

You know I am partial to the opposite sex, Mason.

Precisely.

Thank you, Mason. Have a drink.

Never during working hours, sir, said Mason, lurching towards the door that led behind the bar.

Along with cross-dressing, abuse, self-imposed or otherwise, is *de rigueur* in the Bar, and runs rife. Fingers Smith is known for his unique constitution, having survived years of chemical dependency, while Mad Mack, reincarnation of a namesake thought to have featured in at least two Hogarth etchings, tops the bill and is given latitude, not to say deference, his handshake a threat, his smile an ultimatum.

Yerroirrroit??

No one has ever understood a word of what he says, apart from this simple, rhetorical greeting, his mood and intentions usually

THE FORECAST

conveyed through rumbling of the stomach. Elephants are known to communicate in this way for courting purposes and it is said that Mad Mack once conversed at some length with an African cow in Regent's Park Zoo who had come into heat. For all his powers, his *prowess*, he is unable to order a drink. No matter. Uprights and phoneys alike cater for his every need. If they do not, they may be silenced with a withering look or an obscene, onanistic gesture.

Fingers and Mad Mack are but two elements in that impossibly one-sided equation, through which only a tentative understanding of the conditions is reached. Just how many uprights and impostors, freaks and phoneys, I have remarked, dead or alive, I cannot claim to guess, during my brief, eternal visitation upon these shores, and within the sulphurous ambience of the Bar, yet each, in his own way, either adds to, or subtracts from, the impression I have gleaned of the place, of its character and eccentricity, the whole constituting a dazzling kaleidoscope of the Anglo-Saxon genus. What I can say with certainty is that this gallery of faces and gestures is one which may appear at times to be constant (thus offering a solution of some sort to the algebra of human interaction) but it nevertheless changes, however imperceptibly.

Yesterday (if it was yesterday, for who can tell?), for example, a stranger came into our midst and took to observing my every gesture. How easy it would have been for me to claim that he was dead too! Dark-skinned, with eyes set deeply in mournful sockets, he remained impassive as I stood beside him.

I had entered into conversation with a girl who boasted tortoise-shell eyes and skin of alabaster.

Where do you come from? I hazarded.

A can of Red Stripe, she replied.

THE REAL ILLUSION

Red Stripe?

Lager. Everyone comes from a drink of one sort or another.

They do? And me?

Wine. Burgundy.

Red or white?

Red, of course. No, not Burgundy. Claret. A full-bloodied one. Château Biston.

The year?

Too early to say. But a decent vintage, judging by the way you hold yourself.

Funny how the weather shapes everything.

There's more to it than that. A good vintage is a state of mind. Stars have got a lot to do with it. And the moon. Hold out your hand. Yes. Château Biston. No doubt about it.

The stranger remained perfectly still, fixed within his own orbit, singularly unaffected by the girl's infectious laugh. Now, at last, time faltered, the satellite closing its eye for a moment, tired of its thankless, wholly predictable task, and I turned to face the man, struck by the thought that he had slipped from the pages of a story only half-complete through interruption (I see the author, I see his lover attempting to leave him, I see a typewriter hurled through the window and sent into an orbit all its own). He had begun to talk and I took in what he had to say, still dumbfounded by the girl's honest beauty and poetic nature.

THE FORECAST

"Old Delhi Railway Station" were the words which first registered in my mind. "Yes, a sight for sore eyes. Gold as a commodity was always prized, as it is now in Albion. But where here it is considered a trivial obsession, along with expensive cars, mobile telephones and real estate, in India it was taken far more seriously, for what it was truly worth. Indeed, to be seen trading in it was a capital offence at one time. I recall with the clarity of the dispossessed the sight of young women, their stomachs ballooning under their saris, phantom pregnancies which had resulted from them having secreted the precious metal in their midriffs, yes, incising it beneath their skin so that their bodies became poisoned. Pregnant with gold!"

Such tales are a commonplace in the Bar and one takes them with a pinch of salt, even if one admits that salt is a good deal easier to apply than remove. Judging the amount, therefore, becomes one of the principal conditions laid down for our mutual benefit by the forefathers.

I looked into the eyes of the stranger, who had now resumed his former expression of aloofness. It was as if he had uttered not a syllable and nothing in his stare gave evidence of his having disclosed the slightest trace of character or personality. Could I have imagined it all? Possibly. I looked again at the stranger as he stayed his ground. Behind him, I could see Mason rapping the hands of an impostor with his cricket bat and, to his right, Frank serving White Eye with a half-pint mug of brandy. Beyond them stood the Poet, proud, upright, adjusting his Indian headdress and raising a small aluminium bucket of port to his lips:

"I am a drinker with a writing problem!"

I turned to stub out my cigarette. When I looked up, the stranger had disappeared. In his place stood the Poet, our ghost celebrity, who occasionally surfaces for light refreshment and vanishes, just as quickly,

THE REAL ILLUSION

whenever it suits him. This would be hard to corroborate, of course, as no one else has ever confirmed his presence. Yes, it is because of this simple fact that I remain sceptical, at least as far as ghosts are concerned.

    I stepped out of the Bar shortly afterwards. It was raining, even then. I had the distinct impression, as I do now, that the satellite's dance might have taken it into another orbit, abandoning us all forever, and I can time such an occurrence to that moment at which the stranger remained unmoved by the girl's laughter as he stood there beside me, prior to embarking upon his story. And, now that the satellite has gone, I am convinced Albion will remain forever clouded, forever damp, its terrifying capital justly hidden from view, an alibi for all the crimes ever committed and ever to be committed, long after we are all dead and gone forever. One shouldn't be too pessimistic however. I took the Red Stripe Girl home with me and she has lain in bed with me all day watching me write this, when not staring out through the windows and up to the china-white sky. She has now decided that I come not from a bottle of claret but from something far stronger (*grappa* has been mooted), which, all in all, I consider something of a compliment, for a man of middling age and desperate imagination.

Note: The author acknowledges the declaration "I am a drinker with a writing problem" to the late Brendan Behan.

THE FORMALIST
1995

Everyone has heard of Igor Lassky ("the Formalist") but can anyone say with certainty what happened to him after he left England?

Born in London in 1899, educated at Eton and St Swithin's College, Oxford, Igor Lassky was the youngest graduate of his year and had his first anthology of poems published three days prior to his sixteenth birthday. After serving on the Western Front, where he was wounded (twice) and gassed (thrice), he soon established himself as one of the "Doomsday Set", a group of intellectuals, artists and pederasts within which he exerted considerable influence. His pamphlets on electromagnetism, sado-masochism and "restrictivism" singled him out as a pluralistic genius and one often wonders what dizzying heights of fame and fortune he would have reached had he not been obliged to quit England in 1928, as a result of the "green stocking" scandal in June of that year, a regrettable incident in which his butler, Fred Carling, was found hanging in the broom-cupboard of his house in Shoreditch, naked save for a pair of striped green socks and a Guards' cravat.

Many conflicting theories have been put forward suggesting what might have subsequently happened to Igor Lassky. Some claim that he went to South Africa, others that he chose Lapland, or even the United States of America. Most, however, assumed he committed suicide in disgrace, for how, they argued, could a man of such particular appearance and stature have simply vanished?

At last, I am in a position to set the record straight: the document I have now released for publication is, in fact, the last known letter written by another member of the "Doomsday Set", best known by

THE REAL ILLUSION

his *nom de plume*, Leam Nonis, to Igor Lassky. This letter I found, still sealed, amongst a collection of "Doomsday Set" correspondence and ephemera, which I recently purchased at Christie's. I was also pleased to acquire a photograph of the Formalist, which I had not seen hitherto during the course of my research.

Photographs, as the Formalist used to say, are such "fraudulent fractions"; we compare the subject with that part of a second immortalised on paper, remarking upon differences in the flesh as if they had been corrected, not perverted, by the scientific eye of the lens. According to those who knew him, he never wore anything other than tails, black, patent leather shoes and spats in lilac, his bow tie askew, winged collar jutting out in all directions, hastily starched and always slightly soiled with a fleck of ink or claret, grey, felt gloves and that monocle hanging like a third, roving eye from a yellow cord about his neck. A picture indeed!

Everything about him confirmed his anachronistic nature, as if he were the product of some unique and unfathomable imagination. According to some sources, his face was not nearly as angular as some photographs suggest, the cheeks being rather full in profile, the nose a little more rounded. There was, however, a sharpness to the eyes and brows, as if to reflect the precision and wit of his intellect. This contradiction in his physical appearance symbolised the great complexity of his being and the duality of his persona, a trait often remarked upon by his colleagues and clearly visible in the photograph, yet not so much as mentioned in George Smith's recent *Igor Lassky: A Life in Shadow*.

The letter itself is dated 3 October 1939; the fact that it was returned to sender one year after having been posted may suggest, at first, that Leam Nonis did not, in fact, know of his friend's whereabouts. Its contents, however, which clearly indicate earlier correspondence, put all such doubts to one side, proving categorically that Igor Lassky was alive and well and living overseas from at least 1928 – 1938:

"Dear Lassky, I was very pleased, not to say surprised, to receive your letter. What an age it is since last I heard from you! I had noticed, a while ago, an edition of your most recent opus in the window of

THE FORMALIST

MacBain's in Baker Street, but had elected to await a reply to my last letter before informing you of this. I knew you would be heartened by the news. How clever of you to have succeeded in having it published in London! And how amusing the soubriquet!

"Much speculation has taken place, late into the night, within the dusty confines of London's clubland, as a result of your continued disappearance. It was only yesterday, when I encountered Sir Wystan at the Porchester Baths, that your name was mentioned once again. Yes, Lassky, you are still the 'talk of the town', and anyone who is anyone, it seems, would give the impression that they know of your whereabouts. Sir Wystan thinks you are installed in the Rajasthani hill station of Mount Abu, while Hutchens is convinced you have 'gone West' (as the saying goes) and are currently featuring in a travelling show, following in Oscar Wilde's footsteps, entertaining rustlers and cowboys!

"Poor Hutchens! I fear he is not in full possession of his faculties; the Twentieth Century has confused him terribly (he refuses, for example, to accept the death of Queen Victoria, calling it a 'conspiracy'.) I ran into him outside Quentin's Inner Circle Club: he actually claimed to have received a letter from you, the contents of which, not to mention the postmark, proved unequivocally that you were living in a place called Tucson. Whatever else can be said of you, you certainly manage to remain as mysterious now as you were when you walked the streets of London in the dead of night, speaking to me of your dreams and theories. What an age ago it seems!

"Of course, many people feel that, by vanishing, you seriously implicated yourself in the 'green stocking' affair. The lovebites found on Carling's neck, I must say, do still raise some questions in some quarters, as do the stigmata of considerable voltage applied to the wrist, ankle and genitals. We, who are your friends, however, understand that such injuries could never, on their own, have been fatal (far from it) and we do all we can to clear your name. I dined the other evening with Tristram Ball, whom you may or may not remember from Oxford (he was at St Jude's); he recently won the Liberal seat for Rowington (East) and has promised to do all in his power to help. There is a very strong chance that he will be elected to the Home Office Catering sub-Committee, which I hope encourages you as much as it does me.

"How are you settling in to life in your new surroundings? You stated in your last letter that the natives were very 'open-minded', but what did you mean by this exactly? I can only surmise that they are showing you the deference befitting a man of your stature. Have you managed to master their language, or languages? You did mention that the men of the tribe were 'unusually well endowed'. Are you contemplating some form of ethnological/anthropological treatise on these and other peoples whose paths you cross in your wanderings? Any such observations, I am sure, would be well received. Great minds, as I have often stated, do *not* think alike.

"You will, I know, be sorry to hear that the 'Doomsday Set' is not what it was. There have been a number of unnecessary (in my view) conflicts of opinion. Doddington shocked us all with what he calls his 'new ideas' concerning art. One would have thought that he, at least, would have remained impervious to the temptations of fashion, but having seen his most recent work at the Jefferson Galleries, I must report that we could no longer allow him the privilege of membership. As we stated in our memorandum, if the English landscape isn't good enough for him, then perhaps he should consider other pastures to satisfy his 'modernism'.

"Meanwhile, Stubbings seems to have completely lost his bearings and has repudiated the use of rhyme in his work, claiming it to be 'unnecessary'. If it were unnecessary, I felt bound to suggest, then why had it formed the base of all poetry since man first mused on his surroundings? As for Greenhill, he left of his own accord, which is a pity, I thought, as his last novel, *Fools Rush In*, was a fine effort, if a little inconsequential, even by Greenhill's standards.

"You may well ask, dear Lassky, 'Who is left?' Yes, I will admit that the weekly meetings in Fitzrovia can be somewhat desultory affairs. This is one of the reasons why I feel it so important to keep up the correspondence. Do write soonest and let me know how you are getting on. Peters sends his best. Only the other day he turned to me and said,

THE FORMALIST

'You know, sir, I miss Professor Lassky. He was a gentleman, sir. A veritable gentleman. The staff loved him, especially the younger chaps.'
 "So you see, Lassky, you are not forgotten, not for one moment.
 "All the best,
 "Nonis.
 "PS: I am sending you some of your favourite water biscuits under separate cover."

Much has been said and written about the "Doomsday Set" and the role played by Igor Lassky, but I think this letter reveals more than perhaps any other recent "find". Elsewhere in the bundle of papers I purchased at Christie's, I came across the following text, which I thought worthy of inclusion in this essay. The handwriting is unmistakably that of Charles Benson, the noted etymologist who was, for several years, a close friend of Lassky.

"What a sight he was! Tapping his cane or clicking his heels, the thumb and index of his left hand forever lodged within the dusty confines of his top pocket, anxiously verifying the whereabouts of a handkerchief or the stub of a pencil he might have mislaid five minutes, or five days, earlier, or seeking out the monocle that had dropped to his waist as he raised an eyebrow in amazement at a thought, an intuition, an idea! The left hand would then flicker nervously, producing a Bristol card from an inside pocket as if by magic, the head of the cane would be cupped in his right glove as he finally located the pencil (hidden, for some reason, in the seat pocket of his trousers) and, in a trice, he would be scribbling in English, French or Russian, or perhaps the short-hand he had invented, all the time talking to himself so as not to forget what had occurred to him, an equation suddenly balanced, an aphorism snatched from the overheard conversation of a passer-by. At such moments, the energy coming from him would be prodigious; one could almost see it, pulsating, above his head.

"'Never mistake diet for personality!' he would cry, grabbing me by the collar and making circles in the air with his pencil. 'Even a complete idiot becomes radioactive after eating aubergines!'

"How right he was!"

T.

THE ART OF READING
1985

It is Easter Sunday; I cannot avoid thinking of death, chocolate and rabbits. On the wireless, I overhear a member of a gardening panel declare that he would go "to any lengths" to grow hibiscus. Outside, by way of atmosphere, canoeists, oarsmen, sailors and water-skiers disport themselves on the thick, brown and grey muddied waters of the Thames, competing, for the most part, against the incoming tide. My wife and I remain indoors, silently doing the things we always do. I am at my desk, writing, and my wife has appeared from the living room in order to get a light for her cigarette. I look up at her, so lost to my thoughts it is as if I have never seen her before. I check myself.

On the paper in front of me I have been trying to make sense of the dream she recounted to me earlier, one that, at first, seemed to me to have more literary than symbolic meaning. In my notes, to support this view, I have drawn a parallel with a Borges short story, one of those epic, condensed tales in which the knife used by one of the quarrelling card players assumes its own identity. The knife itself has been used many times and will doubtless be used again; unlike its manipulator, it cannot lose under any circumstances. At least, I think that is how the story, or the dream, goes. I cannot be sure and it is no use asking my wife to corroborate. She only reads fiction in the original, she eschews translation of any sort and, whereas her English, Arabic and Persian are beyond reproach, her Spanish is non-existent. In any case, if my memory serves me, she was reading Robert Louis Stevenson's *The Art of Writing* before nodding off last night. Perhaps, like her, you could think of nothing more symbolic than the suggestion of character in an inanimate object?

THE REAL ILLUSION

She told me that in her dream she had taken the role of the voyeur and that it was I who had been the protagonist. Apparently, I had found myself in a house near Porto, "one of those very grand, crumbling estates you find so romantic for escape and I find so happy to leave…" She smiled. And so did I, if a little nervously.

I had been ushered into a vast, rectangular drawing room, two walls of which were covered in murals of sea battles, and was startled to find that, save for a small desk and a green, velvet-covered chair in one corner, the room was quite empty. There was certainly no human presence, other than myself that is, for the door had been closed behind me as soon as I had entered.

My wife continued. "You walked over to the desk, gazing in wonderment at the painted walls and feeling the floor beneath you sway wildly as if it had become the eye of some terrible storm. On the desk you found a quill with an unusually sharpened point to it, covered not in ink but in blood. With some trepidation, you picked up the curiously stained implement and turned away from the desk, but not before registering the initials 'RLS' on the silver top of the inkwell.

"What you now saw gave you even more cause for concern, for not only had the room begun to move inwards but various cracks had appeared in the marble floor and smoke was billowing from the fireplace to such an extent that you could no longer see to the opposite wall and the door through which you had entered, even as the room itself grew steadily smaller. Along with this, the sound of men crying out in agony, the crack of musket and cannon and the splintering of mast and yardarm now reached your ears, breaking the silence that had accompanied your original move to the desk. You started to scream, like a weasel, and, having lost your footing on the storm-tossed floor, were now lying helplessly between the walls of a room that, to all intents and purposes, had become the principal engagement in some historic sea battle. In desperation, as the walls of the room began to crush your writhing torso, you lunged with the quill, hoping, no doubt, that a change of scene might be effected as a result, wresting you from the

THE ART OF READING

abyss into which fate seemed to have so ineluctably thrust you."

"And then?" I stammered.

"Well, fortunately for you, your deliverance lay in the hands of your alarm clock which, while awakening me with a jolt, left you undisturbed. In other words, you lived to be told the tale. Or slept, rather, while I prepared breakfast."

I am still looking up at her. "You know dreams usually bore me to abstraction. But never yours, of course," I add, hastily. "It reminds me of a Borges story."

"Nonsense, Robert," replies my wife, stubbing out her cigarette in the ashtray on my desk. "You know as well as I do I haven't got round to reading Borges yet. Much as I'd like to."

THE RENEWAL
1985

Before the Renewal, the one that rearranged everything, exciting cartographers and bewildering by-election pollsters (who found themselves voting in a different constituency) we all lived fairly normally. I say fairly because even when things are running smoothly, there is still plenty of mischief to be made. I, for one, was rather disgusted with the *mores* of contemporary life and felt perhaps that the incident I will soon describe was long overdue.

But first allow me to introduce myself. My name is René Tibeau and I come from Paris. At the time, I was living in Milan, that ill-lit city celebrated for its preposterous cathedral and glutinous rice dishes, working as a translator. One fine spring morning, I chanced to be sitting in the study of a friend of mine, Kratch Kratchnik, when all of a sudden, a tremor shook the room. I'd never felt such a phenomenon before, so I wasn't sure at all what it might be. There was some building going on next to Kratch's house, so at first I thought that there might have been an accident or landslip of some sort, but then I knew, almost at once, that that couldn't have been the cause. Besides, it was the wrong time of day for anyone to have been working.

As soon as whatever it was had passed we looked at one another, in silence. Kratch seemed somewhat put out by the whole business, not so much because there might have been some kind of personal risk involved – the building really shook for a moment – but because he had been interrupted. Kratch does not tolerate interruptions. Above us the crystal chandelier swung, casually, making odd patterns around the ceiling and sending particles of dust to the floor. The table had moved

THE REAL ILLUSION

some ten centimetres to my right; involuntarily, I adjusted the position of my chair to make up for the discrepancy. A glass still wet with Barolo had fallen to the floor in pieces and Kratch was shaking his head and muttering Milanese oaths. I felt sorry as only the week before I had accidentally cracked another from the set. Under the circumstances, I felt bound to say something.

"What on earth was that?"

"What? What was what?" replied Kratch.

"But, my dear Kratchnik!" I exclaimed.

"Nothing of importance, René. You need to learn to take these things in your stride."

I looked down at Kratch, wishing he would participate a little more in the drama. "Well, for Heaven's sake, let's go and look at it, at least!"

He stood up himself at this point and walked over to the windows, which were, as usual, darkened by blinds. In a rather tired gesture he took hold of the cord set against the wall and pulled at it.

"My God!" I exclaimed, rather stupidly, as the outside world was revealed to my incredulous eyes. "Nothing of importance indeed!"

I was overwhelmed, for the street outside, the distant cityscape and even the fine spring morning had all been replaced by a picture-postcard view of my native Paris. Instead of via Rivoli, the flower shop across the street, the tram stop and the Lombardian sky filling the window frame, I was now confronted with the very street in which I had been born, the rue Montorgueil. There was Madame Flaubert sitting on a paving stone, begging, Monsieur Gratin selling garlic from an upturned box and there too was Gaston, chanting *"France-Soir! Demandez!"* And, further along, Pierre and Patrick were laughing together at their barrow of household wares. "A dream, perhaps?" I stammered.

"Oh, that's perfect!" Kratch said. "I do so love Paris. Especially in the spring."

This I ignored, opening the window and straining outside to examine the extraordinary phenomenon. Yes, even the smell had changed! I hailed my old friends. *"Pierre! Patrick! C'est moi, René!"* I

THE RENEWAL

shouted. I turned back to Kratch. "Come here, Kratch. Stick your head out of the window. It really is Paris!"

He exasperated me, this strange writer. How could he be so casual about something so exciting? Forgetting him for now, I leaned out of the window again, hailing my friends as before.

"*Pierre! Patrick! C'est moi!*" Maybe the street noise prevented them from hearing me? I shouted again, even louder. And again. Yet neither of them looked up. I tried the others. "*Gaston! Madame Flaubert!*" I screamed. They were nearer to hand. Surely they would hear me.

But they didn't. Or couldn't. What on earth had happened? I began to feel quite shaken.

Kratch Kratchnik had started to laugh. I closed the window and rested my head against the glass, trying to make sense of it all. "Must be just a dream, after all," I concluded. I looked at my watch. It had stopped. Ten-thirty. Did that mean anything? Then I retreated from the window and walked around the room. Kratch had gone back to the table and was correcting the top *cartella* from a pile that made up his book.

"It's the details, my dear fellow. The details that count!" he said, excitedly.

I picked up the bottle of Barolo and poured a healthy measure into one of the remaining glasses. Then I returned to the window to survey the scene. Nothing had changed. Patrick and Pierre were now walking up the street with their barrow. And there was Annette, my childhood sweetheart! How fat she had become all of a sudden! Then I realised. She was pregnant.

"Kratch! What's going on? I don't understand. Not one bit. Is it to do with time? Or place? And how did Annette become pregnant?"

"Drink your Barolo, René. Relax."

"Relax?"

"Yes, plenty more glasses, after all."

I looked at my watch again. To my astonishment, it had started to move backwards, to nine-thirty. I felt a bead of sweat fall from my

THE REAL ILLUSION

forehead. On the wall beside the window there was a calendar. I strode up to it, suspiciously. Not only had the day changed but also the month and the year. So that was it. I was moving back in time!

"For Heaven's sake, René! Relax, I told you!"

I dashed over to the window and slackened the cord. The blind came with a crash and I sighed deeply. It was dark inside the room now, for Kratchnik had elected to blow out the candles after the blind had been raised. I groped my way to the opposite wall, banging my knee on a chest of drawers before finding a match and lighting the candelabrum on the table. What I now saw could hardly have surprised me, for I had braced myself for anything.

Yes: I was back in the nursery at No. 18. And Kratchnik, for the moment at least, had vanished into thin air.

THE RESPECTABLE LADY
1986

When Frederick Whipp first told me this story I couldn't help thinking he was making it up as he went along. On reflection, of course, I realise that not even Frederick would fritter away Happy Hour at the Emerald Bar with such an anecdote if it weren't true. Any story that relies on a preposterous coincidence for its momentum must be true; less improbable happenings are the preserve of literature.

The waiter had just set two fresh Martinis on our table as Frederick embarked on his tale. We usually took it in turns to tell stories, in much the same way as others do to pay for their drinks. The evening before, I had entertained my companion with "The Moslem and The Doubting Christian", the story of two lovers who, having been banished from their respective families "in a multi-racial interpretation of *Romeo and Juliet*", determine to escape their earthly confinement by throwing themselves from Albert Bridge. Moslem tradition dictating that men precede women and Christian tradition dictating the exact opposite, some confusion arises prior to the desperate act, to such an extent that the perverse logic of manners quickly neutralises the fire of passion in their hearts. In short, while recommending a verdict of "death by misadventure", the coroner privately records the likelihood of "simultaneous manslaughter". As for the rest of the story, well, all I can say is that I tried to convey the balance that exists between man's need for sacrifice and his innate capacity for self-preservation.

Frederick received my offering quite favourably, although I could not help but detect a note of sarcasm in his exclamation, "Oh, very good, Oliver! Very good!" Perhaps an air of competition had entered into our storytelling. It's hard to say. Sarcasm has been called the lowest form of wit. For my part, however, there is nothing quite as base, and certainly nothing as humourless, as competition.

Whatever his reaction, Frederick began his story with an air of determination that took me quite by surprise. Tapping a Navy Cut on the lid of his cigarette case, he assumed the sort of expression that presumably indicated the events he would soon unfold would be as startling, if not more so, than the ones which had constituted my own tale.

"George Gilliband" he commenced, "was, to all intents and purposes, happily married. He loved his wife and would regularly inform his friends that he had found the secret to the enjoyment of life. Perhaps that was the problem, the reason he felt the perverse need to experiment and why, one winter's evening, he decided to answer a request for companionship printed in the columns of a well-known periodical.

"*Respectable Lady. Educated. Forlorn. Adventurous. Seeks Gentleman of Like Disposition. No Photograph. No Jokes.*

"The age and qualifications seemed perfect, the very mention of the word 'adventurous' convincing him that here was an ally in experimentation close at hand, a woman after his own heart, so to speak. As I have said" (Frederick had the most infuriating habit of repeating himself) "George was happily married and content with his lot but if there was one negative aspect to his wife Clarissa's personality, it was her lack of adventure.

"Soon enough" continued Frederick, placing his glass on the table and drawing languidly on his cigarette, presumably to add an element of suspense, "with his own credentials sealed and delivered, a rendezvous was arranged in a discreet yet appropriately elegant cocktail bar, not dissimilar to the one in which we are now seated, Oliver. As the day approached, George found it harder and harder to conceal his excitement. What would the lady look like? Would she be beautiful? Above all, would she be adventurous?

"He was in the bar at the appointed evening rather earlier than he would have wished. The table he chose, to one side of an ornamental pillar, gave a view of anyone who entered the premises without making his own presence too conspicuous. In the brief communication he had had with his prospective partner, through a post office box number, it had been decided that he should wear a white carnation and that the lady in question should have a peach-coloured gerbera affixed to her lapel. The suggestion of such an outlandish buttonhole did much to confirm her sense of adventure, even if it conflicted a little with her education.

"The hour of the rendezvous came and went, as it so often does. No Respectable Lady. After twenty minutes had passed, George stood up and walked around the bar. Still no Respectable Lady. Ten more minutes went by. George was dejected. After a further fifteen minutes, during which he stared almost uninterruptedly at the plush green-curtained entrance to the bar, he rose to leave, more angry with himself and with what he saw as a rejection of his adventurous spirit than with his absent date. His mood changed dramatically, however, when he entered the revolving door that separated the intimate warmth of the bar from the London air outside, for there, incarcerated within the opposing, curved triangle of wood and glass, like a waxwork from Madame Tussaud's seen flashing past in a dream, was his Respectable Lady, complete with peach-coloured gerbera, rushing to her appointment. Shocked, George stumbled onto the street, hastily called a cab and disappeared into the night."

"So, he decided not to make the lady's acquaintance after all?" I suggested after an appropriately respectful pause.

"No, Oliver, he did not," replied Frederick, straining forwards to dispose of his cigarette and smiling conclusively. "You see, he was already acquainted with the lady. Only…"

"Only his wife," I continued, "his wife, Clarissa, would have been forty-five minutes late for her appointment."

Frederick looked up, startled. He knew what this meant. Beckoning the waiter, he extracted his wallet and settled the bill. We left the Emerald Bar together, agreeing to meet the next evening. Such was Frederick's mood, I fancy the usual tip was not forthcoming. Our waiter's greeting the following day certainly suggested such an irregularity.

THE ART DEALER
1985

I first heard this story on an aeroplane. There's something about aeroplanes that makes everything fictional; the air of abstraction in the cabin, perhaps. It was wintertime and I was flying to South America, running away on wings. I chanced to sit next to an old man who, at first glance, seemed reticent to engage in conversation but who, with little encouragement, embarked on a lengthy, if diverting monologue. I was playing the devil's advocate, of course, for I usually like to keep myself to myself when travelling. Why did I not do so this time? Perhaps I was acting against my own nature as a test of some sort.

The man told me he had first heard the story a year earlier, while on a flight from Turin to London. "I was seated next to a young man rather like you," he said, dryly. "His name was Carver. Jack Carver."

As the stewardess placed miniature bottles of gin on our folding plastic tables, he apologised for any inconsistencies or gratuitous embellishments that might detract from the substance of the narrative. I replied I was not in a position to judge the story until it was finished and, even then, that I was disinclined to judge anything at all, even fiction. He suggested that age had got the better of him. This too might have been a caprice. I certainly felt he was hiding something.

"Yes, Carver," he continued. "Poor Carver. Or Carvers. Jack and Gerard Carver. One told me the story; the other was the story. You see, Jack was bringing home Gerard's remains in a box in the hold of the aeroplane."

"How shocking!" I exclaimed, hoping to put him off a little.

THE REAL ILLUSION

"Indeed! They were brothers, you see. Gerard was an art critic who specialised in the Quattrocento. Because of this, he spent much of his time in Tuscany. It was on a trip to Florence that he met Salem, a girl of arresting beauty who worked behind the bar in the departure lounge at the airport. Heathrow had been fitted out with new bars and shops situated not in the main departure area but rather at strategic points along the umbilical passageway leading to the gates, presumably to give hurried commuters another opportunity to buy drinks and perfume. Gerard Carver, it seemed, was a young man of fine manners and bearing, but, from what his brother told me, he had recently been ruined by one woman and seemed hell-bent on finding a successor, to assuage his aching heart and possibly exact some revenge into the bargain. The fact that she, at that very moment, was pouring him a hasty gin and tonic was evidently part of some greater plan, similar to the one that has brought us together for this flight to the tropics. You look worried, Mr Lane. I must be a terrible bore for you!"

"Oh no. Not at all. Really. Do carry on," I replied, looking at my watch surreptitiously.

"Examining Salem's face in the way he might have assessed the authenticity of a Quattrocento painting, Gerard Carver smiled broadly, enquired as to her name and, on realising the time, left a tip only marginally in excess of the price of the drink on the bar top. Striding to the relevant gate, he turned back all of a sudden for a final look before entering the aeroplane. "Salem," he said to himself, again and again, as the stewardess led him to his aisle seat in the smoking section.

"Four weeks later he was back at Heathrow, having contrived another visit to Florence. On this occasion he arrived in plenty of time (having curtailed an important lunch at the the Quattrocento Club in Chesterfield Street), savoured three gin and tonics and gazed wistfully over the bar at his future conquest, for there could be no doubt by now as to his intentions. An hour passed thus. Salem smiled at him, sweetly, and said nothing. Gerard smiled back. They created quite an atmosphere for a place not noted for romance.

THE ART DEALER

"A week later, he was back. And a week after that. Fairly soon, the trip to Florence, his research on the monograph *The Quattrocento and Its Greatness* and his professional life in general had all become subordinate to his infatuation with Salem and, like the relationship between the price of the gin and tonic and the tip left behind afterwards, the picture seemed to have lost a certain perspective.

"On the seventh occasion, Gerard Carver asked Salem whether it might be permissible for her to step out from behind the bar in order that he might see her 'whole' as it were. She consented, asking a colleague to take over her duties for a moment. Yes, she was beautiful. All of her. Emboldened, Gerard took her by the arm in a gesture that was surprising but strangely natural and led her to a quieter spot down a tributary corridor and away from the busy thoroughfare that had thwarted the intimacy for which he had so longed. Giddy at the loss of the barrier that had so confined his movements and led his imagination astray on countless, solitary evenings, he stopped her at a suitably darkened point and, after a pause, clasped her in an embrace worthy of any epic finale. That this was a service area at London Airport mattered not one whit, they were in love and love knows no distinctions, of time or place. It can be also rather demanding in its physical manifestations. Some twenty minutes later the pair emerged from the staff lavatory, Salem, in an odd, symbolic twist suggestive of more control over the encounter than she had at first demonstrated, locking the door perfunctorily behind them.

"Gerard Carver had, of course, missed his flight. But that was of little import. He felt flushed with success. Salem remained impassive with just a slight glow to her cheeks. She walked back behind the bar with great serenity and waited for Gerard to order another drink. He ordered champagne and, in a demonstration of vulgarity that would have shocked his closest friends, invited various strangers to join him. This, as they say, came out at the inquiry. The researcher and connoisseur of fine things became quite inebriated, making of his departure a theatrical affair, kissing Salem's hand respectfully before boarding a plane for Milan. The one on which he had booked a seat was, at that moment, landing at Pisa."

At this point in the story, the old man paused in order to take a sip of his drink. For a full minute, he said nothing. To say I felt awkward would be to understate the issue. Finally, his expression changed, his face broken by a sad smile of resignation. It was then that I realised why he had told me the story.

"Naturally," he resumed, "the plane crashed into an Italian lake."

"And the moral?" I asked, more irritated than surprised.

"Moral? There is no moral, Mr Lane. With time, I strive for an understanding of the greater plan."

"And what would that be?"

"Difficult to say. You see, Gerard Carver was my son."

UPTOWN, DOWNTOWN
1996

Hilton was the quintessential New Yorker, born and bred. Along with his elder brother, Bradley, he had inherited two things from his family, wealth and charm, and neither was in any danger of running short. The wealth came from the sale of the family firm at the peak of the 1980s bull market and the charm came from his father who, in the course of a stable and happy marriage, had kept mistresses in five European capitals.

The "third generation" theory claims that while one man creates a business and his son enlarges it, the grandson reduces it to bankruptcy. If Hilton planned on sticking to convention, he certainly had a lot of spending to do, but then Hilton wasn't conventional in the least. Besides, there was simply too much money, so the task was essentially a futile one.

Hilton enjoyed a reputation for eccentricity, which, downtown, is something of an achievement. Since his teenage years, he had made a point of distancing himself from expectation, making of it a priority, so that he often found it harder to decide what to do than what not to do. He had naturally eschewed the destiny mapped out for him by his family, avoiding the professions and moving downtown, away from a job in a law firm and a house on the Upper East Side, both of which so preoccupied his brother. He had instead acquired a vast loft near Union Square, which he had designed and furnished in every detail, as if fully intending to pass the rest of his days in it. He had already lived for twenty years within its industrial, unforgiving contours and, as a result, it had taken on the appearance of a shrine to bachelordom. An artist by default rather than vocation, he spent at least an hour a day producing miniature oil paintings (abstracts mostly) in a studio he kept two blocks from his home.

His adult years were punctuated with cursory love affairs, none of which had marked him. As his parents finally gave up any hope of him ever marrying, he found himself yearning for companionship and true love, and it became an obsession with him.

He lunched once a week with Jackie, his sister-in-law, whom Bradley had married ten years previously. Jackie felt sorry for Hilton and came downtown ostensibly to look at his paintings, which she would occasionally purchase and take back home with her. She was the only person – and certainly the only woman – to take such an active interest in Hilton's life and, as a result, he found himself falling in love with her. At first, Jackie misconstrued his affection for loneliness. She was only partially mistaken, of course. What was strangest of all was that she fell in love with him, most probably out of boredom but also through a different kind of loneliness, one in which she hardly spent a moment alone with her husband, except in that brief period before and after sleep.

As Jackie's guilt got the better of her, she tried to see Hilton on a less frequent basis, but Hilton would have none of it. Over the years, he had drawn apart from his brother, the soaring towers of Midtown effectively creating a barrier between them, and, as a result, he was quite indifferent to the seriousness of the situation. Bradley, meanwhile, had fully understood what was going on – he was a more than competent attorney – and was rather charmed by it, principally because he was not in love with his wife but also because he was conducting an affair with a secretary who worked in an office building not ten minutes' walk from Hilton's loft.

Jane came from Long Island and was an accomplished social climber. She charmed Bradley to distraction and he fell hopelessly in love with her. One day, he called Hilton to ask him whether he could borrow his loft in order to spend the afternoon with her. This was his way of disclosing the affair to his brother, whose guilt he wanted to assuage. "Look, Hilton," he said on the telephone. "I know you're having an affair with Jackie and I couldn't care less. You can use my place."

Hilton had already arranged to spend the afternoon with Jackie so he did exactly what his brother had suggested. Jackie was naturally shocked by the news and could not possibly face making love to Hilton in her marital home. As for Jane, she wasn't in the slightest bit interested in the bohemian charms of Hilton's loft. Being gentlemen by nature, the two brothers swiftly came to an agreement. Bradley would spend the afternoon with Jane in his house uptown and Hilton would spend the afternoon with Jackie in his loft. Creatures of habit that we all are, they soon established a pattern so regular that, within a matter of weeks, Jane had installed herself on the Upper East Side and Jackie had moved, lock, stock and barrel, into Hilton's loft.

Hilton and Bradley became close again, better friends than they had ever been, and they happily resumed their weekly dinners with their parents, heartened by their father's reaction to recent events.

"We never expected you to settle down and find a wife, Hilton. And we never expected you, Bradley, to take a mistress. That the love of your life is already married is a problem, Hilton, that she is still married to your brother, an understandable nuisance. All I can say is that, in terms of real estate, location has always been important. But when it comes to true love, it cannot be underestimated."

THE REAL ILLUSION
1997

The past and the future may well be imaginary but the real illusion, of course, is the present. If you can succeed in holding it, in manipulating it, in bending it to your will, then you will have learned a secret – a trick – only shared by a few. You will also have slapped death such a blow that when he, or she, or it, comes to find you, it will do so with deference. Familiarity breeds contempt, but death, by which I mean time, is not exactly the kindest of allies. Learn, therefore, to play games with the clock even as its hands turn you in ever-decreasing circles. By so doing, you may reach some understanding of your fate.

I have considerable experience of such matters for, at one time, they would pay me to perform magic. I could do many things. I could turn myself into a rabbit and pull myself out of a hat or, with the aid of a fake moustache, pretend to be someone else, reinventing myself in order to earn my keep or cure a broken heart.

I could also do film stars, my favourite being Peter Lorre. People used to say I looked just like him. That was why I kept a photograph of him in my room, as a joke at my own expense or, in the event I had visitors, at theirs.

Is that you?

No.

Who is it, then?

Peter Lorre.

But he looks just like you!

Everyone looks like someone else. Who do you look like?

THE REAL ILLUSION

Yes, they paid me to perform and to look like people. Once, I turned a member of the audience into the Dead Queen, which was a lot harder to do then than it is now. I couldn't turn her back into a member of the audience, so I asked a member of the audience to stand in for her. This went on for a while, until I had run out of audience. So I turned myself into a member of the audience and applauded. The stage was full of Dead Queens and the promoter was furious.

That was a long time ago. Afterwards, my agent got me a job in a film, playing the part of a magician. I waited around on set all day, flirting with the make-up girl. In the evening, I was ushered into a corner of the studio and told to start.

Start what? I asked.

You know. Your act. Start!

I didn't know what to do. The lights were blinding and my make-up began to drip off in beads of sweat, staining my collar. I had never had stage fright before. The director seemed nervous and tired. I looked ahead at the camera lens and then I looked inside myself, checking to see whether I had any tricks there. But I couldn't find any. Time stopped. Nothing happened. The camera turned and I stared at it vainly.

It was then that I started to think of a faraway place at the ends of the earth, a spot over the horizon which was full of everything I had ever seen and, at the same time, empty of any frame of reference, a moment trapped in time for ever, a painting which spread beyond its own frame to encompass all that remained unseen. This place – wherever it was – was the meeting of opposites, it was funny and it was not funny at all, it was empty and it was full, it was sad and it was not sad, it was strange and it was familiar, and I found myself moving within it effortlessly. Yet as soon as I had lost myself to its charms and mysteries, I felt it slipping away from me, like a wave falling back out to sea.

That was great! I heard a voice say, across the gulf that separated me from the camera. I like that a lot! Can you do it again for the reverse shot? I mean, exactly what you just did, or as near to it as you can, I mean, it doesn't have to be exactly as you did it, just as near to what you

THE REAL ILLUSION

did as you can manage, so we can get in a shot of the audience as you see it? OK?

But I hadn't done anything. They wanted me to do exactly what I had done? Or exactly what I hadn't done? When "Action!" was called, I just thought about the faraway place again. I had no idea what I was doing, other than just thinking, that is, but I found I could quite easily slip back into the world I had created for myself. Whatever it was I did, or didn't do, they seemed very pleased with it. As the cameraman and crew applauded, the director rushed forwards and slapped me on the back.

Give the man a drink or something! He's terrific!

BEAUTY AND THE BEAST
2002

THE PRODUCER

"A man of untold ugliness meets a woman of untold beauty. If the man can seduce the woman into declaring her love for him, he will be transformed into a handsome prince." The Producer looked up momentarily from his desk and glanced at the Writer, whose assertive style struck a chord with him, reminding him of his early days, when he pitched ideas to studio executives. "That's eight words more than we usually welcome, but I like it. It's original. Why not develop it further? You know, add some sub-plot to keep up the audience's interest?"

THE REAL ILLUSION

A SIMPLE BINARY FORMULA

The labyrinth is comprised of an apparently limitless number of circular walls. Although haphazard in appearance it is nothing of the sort. Each circle is broken by gaps to the left and right of the point of entrance in the wall facing it. The resolution of the labyrinth accords with a simple, binary formula, a turn to the left, or the right, signified by a 1 or a 0, the whole producing a number which may represent the duration, in milliseconds, of Beauty and the Beast's first, hesitant kiss, or, alternatively, the time taken for a No. 36 bus to traverse the Barra section of Greater Rio de Janeiro, traffic conditions being consonant with a typical Monday morning in summer.

BEAUTY AND THE BEAST

HAMMOCK FACILITIES

Once within the labyrinth, all decisions are irrevocable. Because of its concentric nature and the logic represented by the repetition of gap/wall, gap/wall, it would not, in theory, appear difficult to reach the centre. Do not be fooled. Only your intuition will save you, for all formulae concerning the labyrinth are variable. A momentary lapse, in which you might attempt to reason with what is clearly unreasonable, will result in complete disorientation. Thankfully, refreshments are provided at key locations. Hammock facilities are also available for a small rental fee, the profit from which helps people from developing countries. Your loss is their gain, a comforting thought in the event you never find your way out.

THE REAL ILLUSION

THE BEAST

He was a man of untold ugliness and his ugliness was a part of him. His heart was soft and he cried for the world as he cried for himself, yet he saw beauty in the simplest of things, in the ineluctable force of nature which kept humanity alive and which lit the sky on a winter's evening. No one knew him, his life was a secret, the key to which was lost somewhere. He slept, he awoke, he slept again. He looked into the mirror and he watched a face appear, contorted with the absurd movements a man makes when scraping a razor under his chin, and he wondered at the sight, not to so much at himself as at that reflected world in which he played a part: the world around him, for that is what it remained, around him.

BEAUTY AND THE BEAST

A ROCK THE SIZE OF BELGIUM

He arrived naked into this world. And naked he would leave it. His possessions he had shed and all that he owned, the evidence of a life lived by default, was held in the pockets of his suit jacket. He would drink some drinks and laugh with a stranger, before moving on, to the next memory, and the next day he would discover a book of matches that was not a book at all, but an anonymous phone number on a scrap of cardboard. Such, to him, was man, a finger pointing to some idle evolution, a gesture of animation in a world bereft of sense. Nature herself, with her gifts and thefts, was far too big and important to take notice of him or anyone else, and he laughed at the thought that people might wish to save her, weeping at falling willows and ice melting on the floor. "We are simply waiting for her to take her course," he would mutter in the gloom of another night. "One day, a rock the size of Belgium will fall on our heads and that will be that. It's already on its way, at speed, probably."

THE REAL ILLUSION

BEAUTY

The girl lay upon the bed, quite still, a block of light cast over her body from the window. She lived her dreams and they lived her, her waking life the enactment of hope and loss. She could be racing through time, holding everything dear to her in bags and boxes, or swimming in water that was at once too cold and too hot, or perhaps falling with a building that was a ship caught in a storm. Her beauty was unassailable, her thoughts the inside of a perfect skin. She was alone, alone as she had ever been, but she was not lonely, just vaguely sad, as if she had waved goodbye to a man she had once loved yet no longer trusted. Her life was written, it could be read but not necessarily understood, its myriad interpretations contradictory and ridiculous. She knew it was impossible to analyse anything, that each person was a puzzle with either too many, or not enough, pieces. As for the reading, that could be done in any order, except forwards. Yes, her life was a fiction, as all love stories are a fiction. And her sleep was proof of this, her dreams a constant alibi for existence.

BEAUTY AND THE BEAST

A CURSE

The girl slept on, her breath the exhalation of desire. Beside her, on the floor, was an open suitcase, curious reference indicative of arrival or departure. On the bedside table was a clock, a lipstick, a passport and a book, its title hidden by a glass of water. The alarm was set for an impossible hour; it was just the battery, of course, but she hadn't bothered to change it. She had become indifferent to everything, even her sleep; she disliked her world and she wished to leave it in order to become a new person. In a way, she was tired of her beauty, it was like a curse, vain and useless and rather childish. Within her dreams, she saw herself as plain and unattractive, but, when she awoke and saw her long, blonde hair, the colour of fresh gold, falling to her shoulders, she knew she was the same person who had closed her eyes eight hours before. At the same time, her wild and ragged dreams seemed to age her, taking the years away from her and laughing at her innocence. Was that why she let the clock stand still, its hands frozen as if silenced by a moment of tragedy? To allow herself a chance to get her breath back?

THE HOSTAGE RETURNS
1990

Who knows what lies under my feet? Tall ticklers, stickle-backed giants, the inverted mountain ranges of Mother Earth, bottomless and shady, the wart-necked piddock, the chambered nautilus and the blue rockfish. For, while I plumb the depths of my past, my great white feet plumb the depths of a primordial world lost to all but the scaly-shielded.

I have moved to Paris, yet every time I open my bags, I find their contents have changed. Yesterday, for example, instead of the familiar selection of clothes and objects, I discovered all the relevant garb and accoutrements of the young, French poet, circa 1788 called André Chénier. And, today, amongst an entirely different wardrobe, more contemporary this time, I came across a worn French paperback, which, on closer inspection, turned out to be the first volume of Tolstoy's *War and Peace*.

Circumnavigating the hidden oceans, the Mad Marniks, reincarnation of a thousand drowned sailors, found himself becalmed and near to boiling. After weeks of dehydration and the delirium that only deep anxiety can produce, he elected to douse himself in the thick green waters.

The Hostage returns. At the airport, he is greeted by the President of the Republic, who embraces him with great affection. "Welcome back!" he exclaims to the television cameras. The Hostage looks bewildered, tired and grey. A journalist pushes his way through the crowd: "How did you survive? Did you think of your wife and family?"

THE REAL ILLUSION

Only cursorily apprehensive of distancing himself from his only tangible means of security, to whit his sturdy alter ego made of wood, he shed his ragged clothes and dived in.

The Hostage stares out through slate–coloured eyes. "I found *War and Peace*, he declares, after a long pause. "Part Two. And I read it twenty-one times."

The water, although as hot as tea, revived him, and soon he was swimming with abandon, wheeling his great arms in backward motions, his head held up, facing the empty sky.

I head out into Paris to take some air. After a while, I come across a fire-eater, who is as wide and as portly as a barrel. It is dusk and the fire he holds in his hand burns a thick and liquid orange; orange and black, for the smoke, which is as dark as hell itself, is as much a part of the flame as the hand that holds it.

Time slipped away from him, as surely as the sea-drops from his paddle-hands. Who knows when he felt the first puff of wind against the bristles of his chin?

The fire-eater picks up a small plastic container from the cobbled street and takes in a mouthful of its contents, puts the container back onto the ground, raises his head towards the sky, addresses himself to the flame and, after a long and hollow moment, blows liquid fire up into the sky.

The wind! The wind for which he had so ardently longed! Swimming back to his boat, crying for joy the dusty hymns of his childhood, Marniks suddenly realised the implications of this turn of events.

THE HOSTAGE RETURNS

There is a large, crescent-shaped crowd around the fire-eater. They all look up, heavenward, to follow the line of fire blown from the mouth of the pot-bellied giant.

Whereas, had he been aboard, he would have been busying himself with the rigging, raising the headsail and slackening the mainsheet, he now saw, with horror, that the wind had gained sufficient speed to fill the mainsail and was now propelling the boat at a speed considerably faster than he could swim.

Soon, a smoke ring appears, growing in size with each passing moment.

In no time at all, the boat had disappeared, leaving Marniks quite alone, a speck lodged on a thousand distant horizons.

I follow the ring as it moves on, towards the Seine; shadows dance across the buildings by the river, cast by the spotlights adorning the *bateaux-mouches*.

He swam and he swam and he marched in the slippery water and he became numb and senseless with fatigue, preyed upon increasingly by terrible visions, by the tantalising joys of his past and by a siren who beckoned to him from afar.

The ring has now disappeared, indistinguishable from the darkened clouds of the upper atmosphere.

For eight whole hours he swam and, while he swam, everyone who had ever put to sea made their respective appearances, telling jokes that weren't the least bit funny and laughing at life's tragedy. Even the siren laughed at him as he floated there, adrift.

THE REAL ILLUSION

I move on. The streets are full. Two urchins appear. One offers me a light for my cigarette…

And all the Mad Marniks had in the world, apart from his shrivelled, pulsating heart, was his waterproof watch, which he knew would never stop until long after his head had slipped below the surface.

…while the other picks my pocket.

His legs were weary and heavy as lead but still he kept on swimming. And, as he swam, he could feel something strange against the bristles of his chin.

Now I remember! I had put the Tolstoy in my jacket pocket for some reason. And now it is gone! Furious that something that was not mine has been stolen from me, I give chase.

The Wind! The terrible Wind! Had it changed direction? Or had he? And why now, dear God, had his boat approached on the horizon? Why had it come to haunt him so?

Thinking he might be apprehended, the urchin who picked my pocket throws the book onto the pavement before disappearing around a corner. The other urchin has long since lost himself in the crowd.

He swam with all his might to the boat that had come back to him, not knowing whether his boat was real or not.

I go up to the place where the urchin cast the book aside. But the book has gone.

THE HOSTAGE RETURNS

And, with his giant paddle-hands, Mad Marniks climbed aboard his boat again, looking down at the thick green waters before raising his arms to the sky.

Perplexed, I walk across the boulevard to a nearby café and order a glass of wine. After a while, a man appears, holding a paperback tightly in his hands. He takes a table next to mine and begins reading, turning the pages with thumb and forefinger impatiently. He glances up at me with a smile for a moment. "This one I'm only going to read once," he mutters, half in my direction. "The second volume was a lucky find when I was held captive, but the first volume is priceless."

"I'm saved! I'm saved!" cried he.

Simon Lane was born in England. After graduating from art school in London in 1979, he lived successively in Berlin, Milan, New York and Paris, before settling in Rio de Janeiro in 2001. His poetry, short stories, essays and drawings have appeared in publications throughout Europe and the United States. He has also worked in film, television and radio, as a writer and as an actor. Lane is the author of five novels, *Le Veilleur, Still-life with Books, Fear, Boca a Boca* and *Twist*.

Tunga is one of Brazil's foremost contemporary artists. He has exhibited at the Louvre, the Jeu de Paume and many other museums and galleries worldwide. Tunga and Lane have collaborated extensively on a wide variety of projects.

AUTHOR PHOTOGRAPH BY *Barbara Leary*